BATTLE

OF THE

EXTREMOPHILES

Extremophile: noun: ex·trem·o·phile
An organism that has evolved to thrive in environmental extremes once believed incapable of sustaining any form of life. These extremes include toxic environments, intense heat, cold, and pressure, nuclear radiation, and the profound conditions of outer space.

CRAIG MARLEY

Marine organism images by Phillippe Crassous using Quanta SEM microscope courtesy of Thermo Fisher Scientific.

ISBN-13: 978-1722303884
ISBN-10: 1722303883

Interior design by booknook.biz

TABLE OF CONTENTS

PREFACE

Unlike a prize fight, our oceans didn't die from a single punch to the chin. The battle began with fourteen rounds of devastating body blows - decades of overfishing. This hundred-year pummeling to the belly of Mother Nature caused fish stocks to decline an astounding *ninety-eight percent* while slaughtering a similar number of dolphins, seals, sharks, and turtles.

The knockout punch came in a seemingly innocuous form: *Plastics!*

By the year 2035, billions upon billions of tons of discarded plastics, from water bottles to detergent jugs, from snack packs to baggies, had found their way into our oceans and seas. Over time, UV photodegradation released the toxic chemicals used in the manufacture of plastics, transforming our oceans into highly toxic environments. In the Pacific it was known as The Great Pacific Garbage Patch, and had grown to *six times the size of Alaska.*

Most marine species perished.

A few extremophiles adapted.

Someone had to warn the world of the dystopian consequences.

CHAPTER 1
EATEN ALIVE

2035: Tiki Kalani was a handsome, twenty-six-year-old native Hawaiian. Standing six feet, three inches and weighing two hundred and twenty pounds, his massive chest pressed firmly against the buttons of his multi-colored, short-sleeved Timmy Tigre aloha shirt. A solitary four-inch-long tattoo of a *kakalakeke*, a cormorant, symbolic of health, fertility, and peace, was prominently displayed on his right biceps. Tiki's light brown skin, sea-green eyes, and virile Polynesian physique elicited welcoming smiles from the ladies and a nugget of envy from his contemporaries.

After entering the central shopping district of Lihue, he quickly found a metered parking spot near his father's jewelry store - a vintage two-story white stucco structure located a few hundred yards from the marina. He signaled his intentions to parallel-park his compact Amazon electric pickup, put her in reverse and cautiously backed into the open space. He gave the horn a couple of quick taps to acknowledge a friend walking his dog and announce his arrival to anyone else within earshot. He closed the windows, exited, and stepped away from his new toy, giving her an admiring glance while pressing the auto-lock button on his remote. As he walked away from his silver half-ton, his pony-tailed mane of curly black hair bounced nonchalantly across the pit of his broad shoulders. The sweet fragrance of Kauai plumeria blossoms mixed with a dash of sea spray surfed across his nostrils. "What a splendid morning," he whispered, looking up at the bluest midsummer sky.

Tiki calmly maneuvered down the busy Rice Street sidewalk to his father's jewelry store, dodging skateboarders, shoppers, and sidewalk café patrons enjoying their morning coffee, perhaps accompanied by a blueberry muffin or a bagel topped with cream cheese and a slice of pineapple.

"Aloha, Makani," he said cordially as the portly female acquaintance approached carrying a bag of groceries. Her once lithe figure now filled an extra-large blue and white muumuu. A wide-brimmed straw hat topped her elliptical face.

"*Aloha kakahiaka*. Good morning, Tiki," Makani replied with a constrained smile.

Fifteen years his senior, Makani Nelson had been an attractive teenager who often watched over him and his younger brother while their parents went out for the evening. But now, after twenty years of marriage and two rambunctious teenage boys, her puffy face and sorrowful eyes told the story of a weary, unfulfilling life.

"How are your boys, Hani and Akamu?" Tiki asked, pretending to be interested.

"They're surfing at Kings Beach. They've been there since before sunup. They love to surf and it gets them out of the house while I do my chores. But it's also dangerous. The swells are coming out of the north bringing some big rollers. I worry about them when these big waves hit. The bottom is shallow and covered in coral. Sammy Mola broke his back under these conditions. He's lucky to be alive and back on his feet. How about you? Are you still collecting those beautiful Ni'ihau *pupu* shells?"

"I sure do. It's in my blood, you know. I'm wearing one now. Here, take a look." Using his thumb, Tiki lifted his necklace of black pupu shells off his chest.

"Oh, my God! It's exquisite. It looks great on you too. Did you find these shells? I know they are very rare - must be worth a fortune. Is it true they only find these black ones in Ni'ihau?"

"Yes. These pupu shells are from Ni'ihau." Having the requisite native Hawaiian heredity allowed Tiki to live and work on Ni'ihau, a small, US government-controlled island located eighteen miles off the west coast of the island of Kauai, and the exclusive birthplace of the most desirable and rarest pupu shells. "I got the pupu bug when I was just old enough to walk on the beach. Now, only the ladies walk the beach. They gather the common white *momi* and *laiki.* The rarest shells, hot-pink *akala kahelelani,* and these black ones too - they're outside the reef in deeper water. They come out of their hidey-holes when the sun goes down. That's when I grab 'em - scoop them up by the dozens. Nobody knows about my beach. It's been a secret of mine since I was a kid - you know, when you used to babysit Danny and me."

"You must be rich and famous by now. Do you spend much time on Ni'ihau? What about your father and mother? How's their jewelry business? What's your brother up to? Are you married? Do you have any children?"

Tiki's father, Kane, had the good fortune of being a descendant of the royal bloodline and great-grandson of Princess Lanikai, the youngest sister of Queen Lili'u. As the mayor of Lihue and owner of the most successful jewelry store on the island of Kauai, he led the marketing effort and makeover of the island infrastructure necessary to compete against Oahu and Maui for tourist dollars. His popularity with the locals gave him the support required to attract real estate developers and opportunistic businessmen, all things necessary to grow the local economy and provide good employment opportunities for the resident population. He was a savvy business owner always looking for new opportunities to grow his business, particularly since the island of Kauai was now drawing a significant number of international visitors.

Tiki's mother, Lelani, the eldest daughter of a respected pineapple farmer, was born and raised in Kauai. As a child, she developed a passion for designing and crafting pupu shells into beautiful jewelry. By the time she met and married Kane in 2004, she was regarded as one of the most talented pupu jewelry artisans in Hawaii. As an aspiring jeweler, Kane knew he and Lelani would make a good team and they quickly formed a loving partnership. Their first of two sons, Tiki, was born two years after they married. Danny followed eighteen months later.

"Thank you for asking. My fiancée Koko and I have an apartment here in Lihue. I take my boat to Ni'ihau to collect pupu shells two or three days a week - spend the nights either on my boat or at my brother's place in Ni'ihau before returning. Danny works at the desalination plant. My dad is very busy and doing well. He sells some of my shells in his jewelry store. My mother designs and strings them using only the rarest shells - the ones I gather off my secret Ni'ihau beach. Come with me. I'll give you a quick tour of their store and show you some wonderful strings of black kahelelani and laiki shells. You'd look fabulous wearing one of those."

"My husband Albert would go ballistic if I spent his hard-earned money on a pupu lei."

"Oh, come on, Makani. You deserve it. Take a peek. There must be something that tickles your fancy. And my father will give you a big discount."

"*Mahalo nui loa*, Tiki. Thank you very much. But I must get home and start preparing dinner. We've got company for dinner tonight. Albert is cooking kalua pig and I promised to play a few Hawaiian songs on my ukulele. You know me, always the life of the party. Thanks for inviting me to the store. Maybe Albert will spring for one of your family treasures for my birthday or our twenty-first anniversary."

"I'll be sure to drop the hint if I see him. See ya later. Say hello to the boys."

"I will. I hope to meet your fiancée one day soon. When are you getting married?"

"We haven't set a date; probably next spring. Koko works for the government, the Laser Defense Group here in Lihue. She's a software engineer in the IT department."

"Good for you - getting hitched to someone who understands our digital world. It's getting a bit overwhelming for us older folks, all this high-tech this and that, artificial intelligence, drones, robots, the cloud. I don't understand most of it. Neither does Albert. We're still struggling to figure out all the applications on our smartphones. Heck, if they're so smart, why does it take folks like me so long to figure out how to use them? Everything is moving too fast. Oh, well, I hope to meet her someday. Good luck hunting pupu shells."

****

"Hey, Pop. What's up?" Tiki embraced his father and gave him a hearty squeeze. Kane Kalani revered Tiki, his first son, loved him with all his heart, more perhaps than life itself, and bragged about Tiki's accomplishments to everyone he knew. Tiki inherited his father's build and gregarious personality. He would do anything to please him.

"Damn place is getting to be too much for my ancient bones. The lava in my veins is cooling down. I need a break. And so does your mother. Maybe we'll spend some time at our cottage on Ni'ihau. You got any decent shells for your mother and me?" Kane held out the palm of his massive left hand, nervously waiting for Tiki to reveal his treasures from the sea.

Tiki winked and reached into his right front pocket.

A zealous grin slowly blossomed on his father's face. "Let me see them. I knew I could depend on you to bring me something special."

Tiki removed the small suede pouch from his khaki shorts and slowly unzipped the opening. His father's hand began to tremble.

Moving closer to the long glass display case, Tiki meticulously emptied the contents onto a purple, velvet-lined display dish.

"Holy Mother of God! They're magnificent. Glorious. Breathtaking. Exceptional color and condition." He picked up one of the black shells with his thumb and forefinger and brought it closer to his eyes. "It's perfect. Not a single scratch." He then reached for his eye loupe to inspect the shell under magnification. "The sheen is incredible," Kane asserted.

He replaced the first shell and picked up another, slowly rotating the shell while inspecting it with his optic.

"Tiki, this is the finest lot I've ever seen. I'm very proud of you, son. Wow! You did it, Tiki. You found something rare and of great value. I assume you retrieved these from your secret beach?"

"Yup. That's where I found these. And Dad, there are many, many more, just like em."

"Mother will go bananas when she feasts her eyes on these treasures. How many shells are in this lot?"

"Two hundred and ten, enough for a double-strand lei. What do you think?"

"It should sell for about twenty grand, maybe more, depending on how much gold Mother uses. She will certainly have fun designing a one-of-a-kind lei. Maybe she'll string them with some eighteen-karat-gold beads or rare striped pupu. What do I owe you?"

"Same as the others, ten percent of your retail estimate - half now - half after you sell it. I'm headed back to the island tomorrow. Danny is hosting a BBQ for some of his buddies. I'll be back in a few days with another lot of blacks and maybe some hot pinks."

"Well, son, if the next lot is anything like these, we're all in for some big paydays."

****

"What's the matter, Tiki?" Koko whispered, rubbing her sleepy eyes. "You've been romping and rolling all over the bed since midnight."

"I can't stop thinking about my trip. I gave pop some black pupu shells and he went crazy. I've got to get back to Ni'ihau and grab some more before the weather picks up. I can't sleep - too much excitement."

Koko glanced at the red digits on their bedroom clock. "It's past four. It's Saturday. When are you leaving?" She pressed her warm breasts to his back and traced her toes down his calf and across his ankle. "I'll miss you. Come kiss me. I need some lovin' from my man before you go."

A lubricious smile washed across Tiki's face as he gave the woman of his dreams a tender kiss. "You look so lovely in the morning - very sexy too. I love the way your hair flows over your pillow, like... um… sweet maple syrup." He cupped her left breast and pinched her nipple ever so gently.

Koko sighed. "Tiki. I love you with all my heart. I worry about you when you go off to Ni'ihau. Every kiss goodbye feels like it might be the last kiss we'll ever share. You'll be careful, won't you? I couldn't go on living without you," she purred, then fluttered the tip of her tongue over his ear, down his neck, and across his shoulders. Seductively she purred. Their mouths merged and their tongues commenced to dance a libidinous twist. Koko pulled back, wet her lips til they shone in the pre-dawn moonlight and without a word took charge of their foreplay.

"Roll over, sweetie. Let me warm you up - give you something wonderful to remember during your journey."

Tiki quivered with anticipation. "I love you, Koko. You're so beautiful. You make me feel like a king. My mind tells me not to miss you, but my heart says I must. You're the love of my life."

"Come to me. I want to feel your heart beating deep inside me."

****

"How about jumping in the shower while I fix us a pot of coffee?" Koko asked after wrapping herself in a pink bathrobe.

"Sure. That sounds great. Don't worry about breakfast. I'll get something in Kehaha. I gotta get some gas and provisions before heading out."

"You're staying with Danny, right?"

"Yeah. He's having a party this afternoon with some of his friends from the desalination plant. It should be fun, but I can only stay awhile. Gotta grab some pupus before it gets dark, before the man-eaters go on the prowl, you know, tigers and great whites. I wish you could be there with me. With your beauty and charm, I'd claim all the bragging rights."

"Thanks, honey. Say hello to Danny for me."

****

While in Lihue, Tiki moored his twenty-three-foot Grady-White Gulfstream cabin cruiser at the Kehaha Marina. Located on the eastern shore of Hanapepe Bay, the marina was a thirty-mile drive from Lihue up highway 50. From here, the journey to Ni'ihau would take him thirty miles across the Kaulakahi Channel to the rocky shore of a five-million-year-old volcanic island crater named Lehua. There, he would turn south through the Lehua Gap and make his way along the western shore of Ni'ihau until he arrived at his secret dive spot.

"Hey, skipper. Where you headed?" Poki, the Kehaha Marina manager asked in his gruff smoker's voice.

"If I told you, well... you know what those CIA guys say."

"Sorry I asked. Everyone I talk to around here thinks you've discovered a special place for black and hot-pink pupu shells - the finest and most valuable ever found. You'd better not let anyone see where you're going or you'll have a lot of claim jumpers trying to horn in on your mother lode."

"You won't say anything, will ya?"

"My lips are sealed. Besides, you've always given me a couple of your best shells. I appreciate your generosity and I'd never fuck up a good deal. Don't you worry. Anyone asks, I'll tell them I don't know shit. Maybe you went south, somewhere near Nonopapa Beach. You do have a special beach, right? Walk it at night, during low tide, on the windward side, right? It's got to be windward - nighttime - low tide."

"Like I said, Poki. I'm counting on you to keep our little secret."

After loading his provisions - food, ice, and bottled water - and topping off his fuel tank with high-octane petrol, Tiki fired up the two-hundred-and-fifty-horsepower outboard and checked all the auxiliary equipment - bilge pump, sea cocks, generator, radar, and marine band radio.

"Kehaha Coast Guard, this is *Pupu King*. Come back."

"*Pupu King*, this is Kehaha. Nice to hear from you, Tiki. Are you heading to Ni'ihau?"

"Roger. I plan to be there a couple of days and return about five in the afternoon this coming Friday. How's the weather in the channel?"

"The forecast is for clear skies, three-to five-foot southwest swells, wind from the north, ten to fifteen miles per hour, no precipitation. Sixty-eight low, eighty-four high. Use SSB channel twenty if you need me for anything."

"Thanks. Talk to you later."

"Good luck. Call when you leave Ni'ihau. See ya about five Friday afternoon."

****

It was just after nine in the morning when the *Pupu King* cleared the Kehaha channel marker and Tiki pointed her bow westward. He had made this journey hundreds of times - sometimes on glassy seas - others in ten-foot swells and forty-knot winds. The deep-V hull and high freeboard of the Grady White handled the swells with ease - up one side and down the other. Most landlubbers would find these conditions sickening unless they had numbed their vestibular system with a dose of motion sickness meds. For Tiki, it was just another day on the ocean, in a place and time where he felt he belonged.

He entered open water, set his course on autopilot and broke out a couple of trolling rigs. "Koko would love to sink her teeth into some fresh *ono* or *ahi,*" he muttered. But he knew that was just wishful thinking. Wahoo and tuna were endangered species and the farm-raised knock-offs just didn't have the same texture or flavor. Besides, no wahoo or tuna had been sighted in Hawaiian waters for many years. "Maybe I'll get lucky and catch a mahimahi or barracuda," Tiki mumbled.

As his journey progressed, five-to seven-foot whitecaps came out of the north causing *Pupu King* to abruptly jerk from port to starboard, and limiting her forward progress to about eight knots. Suddenly, a ten-foot roller washed across her bow, sending an avalanche of seawater over the cockpit and breaking Tiki's grip on the helm. He quickly regained his balance, eased back on the throttle to five knots and did his best to maneuver around the biggest swells.

"Fuck this shit," he shouted in exasperation.

A little voice hissed in his head. *"You have no control over the ocean, so shut the fuck up and steer."*

Without warning, the outboard engine stuttered and groaned to a stop as a large swell slammed her port side, knocking Tiki into the starboard gunnel. "Jesus, what the hell is going on?" he cried out, rubbing his aching thigh. "It must be the prop. Something is fouled in the propeller."

He initiated the electric motor, slowly lifting the outboard from the water and exposing the propeller. "Goddamit. Fucking fishnet. These jerkwad commercials don't give a rat's ass about leaving their trash in the ocean. Son of a bitch."

Tiki grabbed a fillet knife and began to cut away the fine-mesh nylon net, taking great care not to accidentally cut his hand in the process. "They must have been fishing for herring or sardines. That's all that's left in these waters." Tiki didn't care if no one heard his complaining, but he always felt better expressing his grievances aloud rather than letting them fester in his head.

The waves continued their onslaught, bashing *Pupu King* and hurling Tiki from side to side. If it weren't for his strength and experience, he'd have been tossed overboard from the largest rollers or impaled by the fillet knife.

The more he cut, the more he came to realize he was surrounded by the algae-coated remains of a huge purse seine.

"Fuckin' thing was probably lost years ago. Probably cast off and sent adrift when the skipper concluded he'd been skunked. He figured it was better to tell the owner his million dollar net was lost in a storm than admit there were no fish left to catch. Shit, there's no end to this fucking net. Maybe I can paddle out. There's no other way."

Tiki pulled out his paddle and began to stroke - four or five counts on the port side followed by a similar stroke count on the starboard. "*Ke Akua pu.* Thanks a bunch, *Kanaloa,* ruler of the sea. Now we're making headway," Tiki yelled facetiously while streams of stinging perspiration rolled off his forehead into his eyes.

As *Pupu King* crept pathetically along the top of the net, Tiki counted his strokes. After a thousand cycles, he stopped for a break and took his bearings. His GPS indicated he had traveled about a hundred feet. However, he was still entangled in the abandoned fishing net and continued to be assaulted by the waves.

After another two thousand strokes, he stopped for a moment to catch his breath. Looking at his watch he grumbled, "Jesus Christ! It's almost two o'clock. I'm going to miss Danny's BBQ. I better keep up the pace. Ain't nobody goin' to save my ass except yours truly."

It was a long and painful afternoon. After paddling his five-thousand-pound cabin cruiser against the forces of confused seas and the grip of the abandoned fishing net, Tiki finally earned his freedom. Battered and bruised, he was thankful to no longer be imprisoned in the purse seine.

"*Mahalo, Kanaloa.* Thank you," Tiki shouted as he fired up the outboard. Exhausted and dehydrated, he gulped down a bottle of cold water and continued toward his secret dive spot.

****

He entered the calmer waters of the Lehua Gap about six. The sun was creeping toward the horizon. It had been one of his most tiring and time-consuming crossings. It was time to rest, cruise the last few miles, and drop anchor over his secret dive spot.

"Hey, Danny boy," Tiki spoke into his cell phone. "It's me. Listen, my engine got fouled in a big fishing net and I've spent damn near all day paddling to get free. I won't be able to make it to the party. I've got to take care of business. I'll swing by your place after dark and spend the night. Okay?"

"Man, you missed some good kalua pig. Shot it myself, a hundred pounder. Tender as chicken. Sorry you got hung up. Suki and I will be up when you get here. There's plenty of pig left, cold beer, and some wonderful mangos too."

"Great. See you later." Tiki disconnected the call and focused on the pupu hunt.

It was close to seven when he reached his destination. Tiki reduced his speed to maintain steerage and diligently watched his GPS while simultaneously navigating *Pupu King* around the shallow coral heads and lava tubes, either of which could easily put a nasty hole in the belly of his livelihood. When he reached his pre-programmed GPS coordinates, he killed the engine and immediately dropped anchor. After paying out a hundred feet of nylon rope, *Pupu King* settled downwind, a short swim from his secret lava tube. The sinking sun remained a few degrees above the horizon but there was still plenty of daylight to see inside the lava tube.

Tiki secured his facemask and jumped feet-first into the sea. The sudden surge of cool water followed by the tickling sensation of rising bubbles dancing across his chest took him back in time to when he first discovered this magical place.

****

Tiki and his younger brother Danny had been searching for pupu shells on Keawanui beach at the north end of the island when he spotted a huge black and white cormorant free-falling from the sky - his long neck stretched to the limit, his pointed bill ready to impale an unsuspecting fish. As the voracious raptor zeroed in on his prey, he folded his wings next to his body to make a clean entry into the sea, then spread his wings to fly through the water toward his prey, diving as deep as forty feet to impale his dinner.

"Look, Danny! A cormorant. They're sent from heaven, a gift from God. Look at him dive. Isn't he beautiful?"

"Come on, Tiki. Stop wasting time. We have to head back to the cottage soon and I don't have a single shell to show Mama or Papa."

"That seabird is a messenger - a messenger from heaven. He's trying to tell me something - something wonderful. Look, see where he dove. There he is, on the surface. He's got a fish too." Tiki shouted, pointing to the bird swallowing his dinner in a single gulp.

"You can bird-watch all night for all I care. I'm heading home." Danny turned and walked back to where they had parked their bikes.

Believing strongly that the cormorant had delivered a secret message, Tiki decided to check it out. He grabbed his facemask from his backpack and dove into the shore break. Once past the breakers, he swam over the reef to where the cormorant had entered the ocean. Here, the depth was about twenty feet. The sandy bottom rose up from the abyss until it washed against the lip of a lava outcrop deposited by an ancient eruption.

He took a few deep breaths, and then swam toward the bottom using his powerful arms and legs. During his descent, he followed the wall of solidified lava until he reached the chalky-white bottom. Changing direction, he swam a few yards along the face of the outcrop, descending to a depth of almost thirty feet. It was here that he caught a glimpse of a dark opening in the lava wall near the seafloor. Like a castaway discovering an island, to his surprise and jubilation, he had discovered a lava tube, a small cave with an opening just large enough for a man to enter. He had learned all about lava tubes in school and how they were formed from a river of molten rock during a volcanic eruption.

Resting his bare knees upon the fine-grained sandy bottom, he cautiously lowered himself head-first into the narrow opening so as not to be cut by the sharp lava or spook a toothy moray eel from its lair.

It was dark inside - as dark as a moonless Ni'ihau midnight. But after a few seconds, his eyes adjusted to the darkness and he was able to define some of the interior features. The cave extended far beyond the opening, but it was too narrow for him to explore more than the first few feet. The walls were covered in leafy green algae as far back as he could see. The bottom was covered in sand and - to his astonishment - dozens of black pupu shells.

Tiki picked up the nearest one and examined its metallic sheen and luster. He grasped another, identical in size and beauty to the first. In need of a breath, he quickly surfaced holding the treasured black pupu shells. He placed them in the pocket of his shorts, took in a fresh lungful of air and returned to the lava tube. Dropping to his knees, he lowered his torso into the cave and scooped up a few more black shells.

With daylight dwindling, he decided to make one more dive, this time to disguise his thrilling discovery. Upon reaching the bottom, he found a large freestanding piece of dead coral. It took a second dive, but he managed to position the heavy block of coral a few inches inside the lava tube, blocking its entrance.

By the time he surfaced, the sun had disappeared below the horizon. Colorful bands of red, orange, and gold clouds spanned across the sky from north to south. It was time to go home and hungry sharks would soon be on the prowl.

As he rode his bike down the hard-packed trail toward his island home, he thanked the cormorant for blessing him with such a special gift and promised the sacred bird he would forever keep his gift a secret.

****

Before diving into the ocean, Tiki double-checked his anchor, making sure *Pupu King* would not drift off while he was in the water. He spat a glob of saliva onto the glass faceplate and rubbed it over the surface to keep it from fogging up. After securing his nylon belt and shell pouch around his waist, he positioned his facemask and jumped feet-first into the sea.

As the bubbles dispersed, the bottom came into view thirty feet below. It would have been much easier and much more productive to use scuba tanks, but scuba gear was forbidden on Ni'ihau - not just for hunting shells, but for any form of underwater fishing. If caught, he would be fined and lose his pupu fishing license.

Tiki swam along the surface until the familiar contour of the lava wall came into view. He looked to the left and right, confirming his location, then inhaled and exhaled several times to rid his body of carbon dioxide. Taking a deep inhalation, he swam head-first, using his powerful arms and legs until he reached the bottom. Here, thirty feet below the surface, his oxygen reserves would allow him to stay for almost three minutes.

The entrance to the lava tube was exactly as he had left it a few days earlier, one large chunk of dead coral, surrounded by several smaller pieces. Tiki was proud of his camouflage and thought it was a masterpiece of deception. After all, this lava tube was not only his discovery and his secret; it was also his sole source of income. He knew if he and Koko ever married, he'd need to provide a comfortable life for her and their children. His discovery had never failed to yield a substantial income and Tiki took whatever means possible to keep it a secret and protect it from intruders.

He pushed and pulled the coral blockade he had placed until the narrow opening to the lava tube was fully exposed. He then settled his knees onto the chalky-white sand and slowly lowered his torso into the cave as he had done hundreds of times in the past.

Seconds later, he found his first black pupu shell - followed by another, and another. As he retrieved each shell, the intoxicating thrill of his discovery intensified.

But how and why did these gastropods come to inhabit this magical place? Tiki thought about it all the time, but still hadn't figured out why these creatures with shiny black shells happened to thrive inside this particular lava tube.

Unable to penetrate more than a few feet inside the entrance, he could only guess as to how far the tube extended - twenty, fifty, maybe a hundred feet or more. There must be, he believed, a huge colony of black pupus living deep inside. They surely had all the food they needed and protection from predators. And perhaps before they died, he mused, they migrated to the entrance for him to gather their beautiful shells, liberating their spirits to a fulfilling afterlife. Upon further reflection, he came to a solitary conclusion. Only the cormorant knows.

With a half-dozen shells secured in his pouch, Tiki surfaced to renew his oxygen supply. Satisfied that *Pupu King* was holding fast to her anchorage, he took several deep breaths, dove back to the lava tube and settled his knees onto the chalky-white sand. He reached as far as possible into the tube and discovered several shells, but he spied several more only inches from the tips of his fingers. Obsessed, Tiki focused all his senses on gathering these more distant specimens. Determined to reach farther back into the lava tube, he squiggled and squirmed, leaving small pieces of his flesh on the walls of the lava tube.

With his mind and body preoccupied and a trickle of blood oozing from his wounds, Tiki didn't see or feel the shimmering translucent mass gracefully emerge from a depression in the seabed. As the cloudlike mass rose up from the bottom, it gave birth to hundreds of miniature cyclones - each one containing a colony of translucent organisms - thousands upon thousands of them.

As they swirled, the colonies emitted random pulses of iridescent blue-green light, communicating information from one colony to another. Each colony swirled and moved in unison, as a coordinated unit, like a giant school of sardines. Stealthily, the near-invisible mass effortlessly moved up and over Tiki's bare skin until his feet and legs were completely engulfed up to his thighs.

Seconds later, a jolt of pain shot up his legs. Tiki jerked violently from the excruciating burn of what he imagined to be thousands of stings from some kind of marine creature. Overwhelming pain rose from his feet to his thighs - intensifying with each passing second. His first thoughts fixated on what kind of creature could create such agonizing suffering. Fire ants came to mind, but he knew that was not possible. His brain then surmised he was the victim of a large jellyfish. No, he concluded. Jellyfish don't attack humans.

Outraged and filled with adrenaline, Tiki struggled to extricate himself from the lava tube. In his haste, he received several cuts on his hands, arms, and chest. He pushed himself free and was instantly overcome with fear as he gazed at the carnage. His feet and legs were covered in a swirling, translucent mass of miniature cyclones. Blood oozed from his feet and legs as a plethora of hungry mouths cut deeper into his flesh.

Tiki suddenly realized he was being drawn down, like quicksand, into a depression in the sandy bottom. He tried with all his strength to free himself, but the harder he pushed, the further he was drawn into the depression. He kicked and thrashed with all his might, determined to escape this abomination. What the hell is causing all this pain? What kind of demon is attacking me? Bolts of confusion exploded across his mind.

But time was running out - his strength was depleted. He needed to breathe. He needed oxygen, and he needed it now.

The spinning mass continued to pull him down, feet first, flashing iridescent lights, feverishly sucking him deeper and deeper, while thousands of tiny voracious mouths consumed his flesh, cell by cell, until the image of his beautiful Koko appeared one final time before he lost consciousness.

What he did not know, nor would he ever know, was that he had been eaten alive by a legion of extremophiles, an organism that quickly evolved to thrive in environmental extremes - environments incapable of sustaining most other forms of life - a creature that likely came to earth locked inside an icy asteroid, comet, or meteor billions of years ago - a creature that has survived every major extinction event including the Cambrian, Permian, Triassic and Jurassic, *each of which wiped out up to ninety-six percent of all life on planet Earth.*

****

On the fourth ring, Koko abruptly sat up, rolled over and picked up the receiver. "Hello," she said, wiping her eyes. "Who's calling? It's past midnight."

"Koko, it's me, Danny. Have you heard from Tiki? He called me this afternoon and said he was running late. He got tangled up in a big fishing net. He said he was going to hunt for shells and would be spending the night. I haven't heard from him since. I called his cell several times, but he didn't answer."

"No. He didn't call. I've not heard from him. What do you think happened? Maybe he had engine trouble?" Koko began to think the worst. "God, Danny, I just had a haunting dream about him. I saw his face, a sad face. And it was blurred by a misty white cloud. His image gradually dissolved, leaving the white cloud. Oh, God, I hope he's okay." Koko began to sob.

"Hey, don't cry. He's probably fine. You know Tiki. He's invincible - strong and fearless. If you don't hear from him by sunrise, give me a call and I'll go look for his boat. You go back to bed. I'll call the Coast Guard and let them know he might be adrift. Maybe they'll find his boat using one of their satellites."

"Okay, Danny. But I won't be able to get back to sleep. Thanks for calling. Say a prayer for Tiki."

"I will. Goodbye, Koko. Talk to you later."

Danny jumped in his pickup and headed north along the coast road toward Keawanui beach. As he traveled along the cliffs, he scanned the coastline, but there was little moonlight and he could not see past the shore break. After a short ride up the coast, he decided to return home and call the Coast Guard.

****

"Hello," Danny answered on the second ring. "This is Danny Kalani. Who's this?"

"Mr. Kalani, this is Lieutenant Victor Wynn, US Coast Guard. I'm returning your call regarding your brother. I think we've found his boat. Can you confirm the vessel type and name?"

"It's a Grady-White, about twenty-four feet, named *Pupu King.*"

"You might want to check out one of our satellite hits. It might be your brother's boat. She's lying at anchor about two hundred yards off Keawanui beach. We couldn't tell if anyone was on board. Call me back if you need any further assistance."

"Thanks, Lieutenant. I'll check it out."

Koko was at her computer terminal sipping her first cup of morning coffee when her phone rang.

"Koko, Danny here. The Coast Guard found *Pupu King* but couldn't tell if anyone was on board. I'm headed to Keawanui beach with scuba gear and a dive buddy."

"Now I'm really scared. He has a cell phone. He would have called if he was in trouble. Maybe the battery is dead. Oh, God, I hope he's okay. I'm confused. Is there anything I can do?" Koko began to weep.

"Hey, girl. He's fine. We both know he's a survivor. Don't worry. I'll let you know what's going on. Give me a few hours, okay?"

"Well, he'd better come home to me or I'll be royally pissed. Good luck, Danny. Call me as soon as you find out where he is." The haunting vision of Tiki's face surrounded by a misty cloud crept back into her mind.

****

"Yup, there she is. *Pupu King*, anchored just off the beach just like the Coast Guard said," Danny said to his dive buddy, Billy Hatchet.

It was a few minutes before noon when Danny parked his truck and the men clambered down to the sandy beach with their diving equipment. Danny and Billy donned their scuba gear and entered the water. The surf was moderate and they both easily swam beyond the shore break. Upon arriving at *Pupu King,* the men began banging on the hull with their fists.

"Tiki! Hey, Tiki. Wake up, man. What the fuck is going on?" Danny screamed. "Hey, dude. It's Danny and Billy. How about dropping the ladder?"

"Maybe he got drunk and passed out?" Billy speculated.

"Tiki doesn't drink. Here, hang onto my gear. I'm going to climb aboard - see what's happening." Danny removed his scuba tank, weight belt, and fins and climbed up the outboard engine to the main deck. "Tiki. Wake up. It's Danny. Wake up."

Danny opened the door and peered into the empty cabin. "Hey, Billy. Tiki is not here. I found his cell and the battery is full. His scuba gear is here too. Fuck! Where the hell could he be? Come on. We'd better see if we can find him. He's probably nearby." A trickle of despair flushed across Danny's shoulders. He jumped back into the water and secured his scuba gear. "He's got to be nearby. He wouldn't be too far from his boat. Let's start here. You ready?"

"All set. See ya on the bottom."

Danny and Billy were experienced, open-water divers, trained to conduct rescue searches and body recovery. They were both certified volunteer divers for the Kailua Fire Department and had been on several emergency rescue operations, mostly to save or recover people who disregarded small craft warnings.

Upon reaching the bottom, Danny signaled for Billy to follow the lava wall to the south while he searched north. They would meet where the lava and sandy bottom merged.

Danny worked his way down the face of the outcrop until reaching the bottom. He turned north and began to swim, slowly scanning his field of view from left to right. God, this place is desolate, he thought, recalling how things had so dramatically changed over the past decade. This is where Tiki and I used to spear grouper and jacks all day long. Christ, the reef is dead - not even a crab or starfish. What happened to all the sea life? It was a distressing thought.

As he made his way around a large outcropping, he spotted something out of the ordinary. From a distance of forty feet, it looked like a large oval soccer ball resting on the sandy bottom. He picked up his pace, eager to inspect this mysterious object. The closer he got, the more he discounted the optimistic options and began to believe the worst. He approached from the rear and nervously swam to the left.

"No, no, my God, no!" Danny screamed through his mouthpiece. A cascade of bubbles carried his unheard words to the surface. He had come face to face with a human skull resting upright atop the sand, the vertebrae disappearing into the sediment. A black rubber facemask covered the eye sockets. The bones of the left and right arm and hands were spread out atop the sand like the wings of a soaring eagle.

Danny jerked back, horrified at the sight of the bleached skeletal remains. It was a ghostly, deeply disturbing scene.

Danny took out his knife and banged on his tank hoping to get Billy's attention, and then turned back to the tragedy before him. Upon closer inspection, Danny discovered a Rolex Submariner encircling the left wrist of the skeleton. At that moment, he knew these were the remains of Tiki. Seeking absolute confirmation, he turned his attention to the skull, poking the blade of his knife into the sand near the jawbone. Moments later, he carefully retrieved a string of black pupu shells from the sand.

Seconds later, Billy arrived on the scene and was overwhelmed by the sight. He looked at Danny with tear-filled eyes, cupped his hands in prayer and shook his head from side to side trying to reconcile the loss of his good friend, now reduced to a skull and a few bones partially buried in the bottom of the ocean.

The image of Tiki's skeletal remains lying on the bottom of the sea burned deep into his memory bank, Danny was particularly distraught at having to tell Koko that Tiki, her lover, and best friend, was not coming home. He lost his life doing what he loved. All that remained was a string of black pupu shells and his legacy.

CHAPTER 2
CHUUK ISLANDS

Willow Parker abruptly awoke from the roar of the diesel sweeper as it trudged along the beach raking rubbish that had been washed ashore during the previous high tide. Rolling onto her stomach, she buried her head under her down-filled pillow in a meager attempt to block the offensive dissonance from the ten-ton yellow monstrosity. A gentle onshore breeze propelled the pungent essence of diesel exhaust across her olfactory senses while masking the fragrance of the large plumeria tree that graced her beachfront residence.

The sun was a few degrees above the horizon, giving the sweeper driver a clear view of his route along the beach. Luminous beams of Hawaiian sunshine stretched across Willow's bedroom irradiating grains of dancing dust and smoke. It was a midsummer Saturday in the seaside village of Waimanalo on the island of Oahu.

"Damn, that thing is a rude way to start the day," she muttered, burrowing her head deeper into her pillow.

After a few minutes of respite, she threw the pillow aside, ruffled clumps of her dirty-blond hair with both hands, and ambled to the sliding glass door facing the beach to appraise the massive amount of garbage littering the beach. Gazing through the black exhaust of the sweeper, she began to follow a small gathering of sandpipers running willy-nilly in and out of the ebb and flow of the waves, poking their long bills into the sand searching for their favorite prey - bloodworms.

Willow knew all about bloodworms. These segmented carnivorous worms thrived in the wet sand and packed one hell of a bite. Most species were not more than an inch or two long, but the most dangerous variety grew to about two feet. Their powerful jaws contained four hollow pincers that injected toxic venom, quickly killing their prey. Their bite was also dangerous for humans. Like a bee sting, it often triggered anaphylactic shock. As a teen, Willow had experienced a painful, life-threatening encounter with them - a terrifying moment she forever remembered.

One day, while resting on the wet sand on Hanauma Bay, a bloodworm snaked its way from under the wet sand and attacked her thigh. Screaming in searing pain, she jumped to her feet and stumbled across the sand toward the lifeguard station, where she collapsed. As the venom raced into her central nervous system, her throat began to swell and her blood pressure dropped to dangerous levels. She was rushed to the hospital where the doctors administered multiple doses of epinephrine antihistamine.

****

Willow hadn't aged a day since she turned thirty-five, twelve summers earlier. Her delicate features, sensual smile, honey-colored skin, and a figure most women craved, could be intimidating to both genders. But the most noteworthy part of her persona was the world-wide respect she had earned as a marine biologist and environmental scientist.

As Willow took off her nightgown and entered the shower, she drifted back to a time long ago when she was a youngster living in a once-upon-a-time wonderland called Waimanalo Bay. To Willow, it was the most beautiful sanctuary on the island of Oahu. She vividly remembered her family and friends packing a picnic lunch and heading to the beach where they could swim and snorkel surrounded by thousands of colorful reef fish in a perfectly transparent ocean. As she swam over a barrier of ancient corals, she recalled counting the number of parrotfish, angels and damsels, turtles, eels and an occasional *humhumanukanuakapua'a.*

Back in the good old days, numerous travel magazines had named Waimanalo the best beach on the planet, equating it to a tranquil Elysium for families, children, lovers, kayakers, and day sailors. The pristine shoreline was populated by rows of coccoloba, sea grapes, coconut palms, and a few ancient banyans that provided a secure roosting place for whistling songbirds. Beyond the trees, a field of grass and a row of plumeria trees marked the boundary between the beach and Waimanalo Community Park.

By the time she started college, the tourist business had exploded, reaching far beyond the capacity of Waikiki. Unavoidably, the state took advantage of the revenue opportunity. Using its right of eminent domain, it privatized much of Waimanalo Beach and Hanauma Bay - then leased the properties to tour companies for a handsome annual fee.

Tens of thousands of tourists - men, women, and children - were bused from the Waikiki hotels to the private parking lot where a tropical garden once thrived. Here, the tourists paid a hefty premium for the right to trample over the reefs from sunup til sunset while feeding the fish a diet of chemical pellets dispensed from rows of coin-operated vending machines.

Twenty years later, there was nothing left but a lifeless reef. Human avarice and reckless disregard for the natural beauty and ecological magic had gradually turned the reef from an enchanting wonderland into a bleached wasteland. While the tour companies made millions sucking the last whisper of life from the delicate biosphere, the ancient coral reef was trampled to death. The bottom became contaminated with toxic waste from tons of chemical fish pellets and human garbage. Thousands of fragile species of marine life disappeared. By 2025, Willow's Shangri-la ceased to exist.

****

While in graduate school at the University of Hawaii, Willow imagined falling in love with a tall, handsome Prince Charming. But the right combination of packaging, brawn, and brain seldom materialized. Most of the men in her life were no doubt handsome but lacked the necessary maturity or intelligence to make a lasting impression. And she vowed to never lower her standards.

After earning her PhD in marine biology and securing a faculty position as an associate professor, she had little time for socializing and zero time or tolerance for nurturing a relationship. Her work became her master and her mission in life. As the years passed, most of the credible bachelors had fallen for more accessible women and she lost interest in playing the dating game - that is, until she met Blake Reynolds.

****

One summer day, Willow and one of her PhD candidates, Christy Daniels, planned a research dive trip to the Chuuk lagoon, sponsored by the recently established Makai Institute of Marine Technology, a commercial enterprise owned by the University of Hawaii, located on the shores of Waimanalo Bay.

In addition to being the Chief Technology Officer for the Makai operation, Blake Reynolds was the field trip organizer and Divemaster for the Chuuk research project. They were scheduled to make several dives and produce a video record of the marine biomass growing on Japanese warships that had been sunk in the lagoon, formerly known as Truk.

During World War Two, these islands were the main base for the Japanese navy and the most fortified area in the South Pacific theatre. Eleven major islands and forty-six smaller islands encircled the lagoon. It was from here the Japanese launched offensive operations against Allied forces in New Guinea and the Solomon Islands.

Hundreds of Japanese battleships, cruisers, destroyers, tankers, cargo ships, gunboats, minesweepers, amphibious landing craft, and submarines were anchored in the lagoon were. In particular, *Yamoto* and *Musashi,* the largest battleships ever built, were stationed at Chuuk.

In 1944, American carrier-based fighters destroyed the base, sinking dozens of Japanese warships. Chuuk lagoon became the biggest graveyard of ships in the world and a rich underwater amphitheater for marine biologists and adventurous divers.

****

The six-hour flight from Honolulu to Moen City, the capital of the Federated State of Micronesia and largest city in the island country, gave Willow and Christy an opportunity to get to know each other on a more personal basis. Although Willow was her professor and twenty-five years her senior, they were friends and shared many of the same aspirations, including their choice of apparel. So it was not surprising to see both of them admiring a rack of bikinis at one of the local retailers shortly after their arrival.

"Helllooo," Christy squealed, scanning the near-naked manne-quin. "Now that's what I call a bikini."

"You call that a bikini? For crying out loud, there's not enough there to cover up the hot spots."

"Awe, come on Willow. You gotta live life on the edge once in a while. This number would look absolutely *maarrvellouss* on your sexy frame. All those polka-dots. Shucks, girl, you'll drive the men nuts trying to count them all. Come on, at least try one on. I bet you'll love it."

Willow rolled her eyes and shook her head. "You must be joking. I'm too old for showing off that much skin."

"Well, I love it. And I'm going to try it on."

Christy strolled into and out of the changing booth in less than five minutes.

"What do you think?" Christy posed like a fashion model.

"On you, it looks great."

"You really should try one on. I just know you'll love it. And besides, you never know when you might meet Mister Right. You don't want to pass up an opportunity to make his head spin."

"Okay, but I get to make the final decision."

****

Dressed in fashionable itsy-bitsy teeny-weeny polka-dot bikinis, flip-flops and braggadocios straw hats, Willow and Christy lurched down the pier toward the dive boat carrying hefty bags of their personal dive gear. Christy's bikini was white with blue polka-dots. Willow's was the exact opposite.

As he secured the last of three scuba tanks with a loop of bungee, the weathered mariner looked up, intuitively knowing the two approaching ladies were his passengers.

"Good morning, ladies," the man said, taking off his sunglasses, his blue eyes riveted to their saucy attire. "Welcome to Chuuk and welcome aboard *Goldilocks*. I'm Captain Henry. But you can call me Hank or skipper. "

Henry hadn't had the pleasure of entertaining two beautiful, nearly naked American ladies since who knows when. "I see you've been shopping at Lulu's - bought matching uniforms. Which one is for the home games?"

For a moment, Christy didn't comprehend the gist of his levity. After a long pause, she replied, "Oh, you mean our bikinis. Yeah, we thought they were kinda cute."

"Hand me your dive bags. I'll put them here, by the transom, out of the way. Let me guess." Looking first at Willow he surmised. "You must be Willow, and you, young lady," he said, turning to Christy, "must be Christy. Take my hand and climb aboard."

"Thank you, Hank...er skipper," Christ replied with an accommodating smile.

"Either of you want a bottle of ice water or soda?"

"Ice water if you have it," replied Willow, taking a seat on the fiberglass gear locker.

"Me too." Christy grabbed her hat as an offshore breeze caught the brim.

"Been to Chuuk before?"

Willow jumped at the opportunity to proffer her credentials. "I've never had the pleasure. However, I have dived all the Hawaiian Islands, Palau, Australia, Indian Ocean, Caribbean, and the Mediterranean. How long have you been here?"

"Too long, and not long enough. My wife and I came here on a vacation twenty-two years ago. While cruising in the lagoon, she had a heart attack and died in my arms. I buried her at sea. We didn't have any kids so I decided to stay and keep her company."

Willow and Christy shared a quiet moment of bereavement.

"That's a wonderful love story," Christy whispered.

"Hey, life goes on. Oh, here comes the boss, Blake Reynolds. He's smiling. That's a good sign. If he's smiling, we'll have good weather."

Blake walked the length of the boat dock like a full-bird colonel, shoulders back and chest out, his black dive bag in one hand, a first-aid kit and laptop satchel in the other. He wore black bathing trunks, a white sleeveless tank top, a blue baseball cap, and weather-worn canvas deck shoes.

"Ahoy, mates. We've got ourselves a beautiful day for a wreck dive. Hello, Miss Parker," he said with a broad smile. "I've heard much about you. It's great to meet someone important. I've read some of your reports and proposals. Your reputation as a scientist and visionary has made you an international legend and a moving target for some envious fools."

"Well, thank you, Blake. It's a pleasure to meet you too. I understand you've taken a new position at Makai. I've recently joined the Makai team as well. I guess we'll be seeing a lot of each other. This is one of my post-grad students, Christy Daniels. She's working on her doctorate thesis in marine structural mechanics. I thought she might offer a fresh perspective on the long-term effects marine life has on inorganic materials."

"That's an excellent idea. Naval architects are always looking for material science to pave the way to the future. And yes, after fifteen years designing submarines for the government, I've accepted a position as Chief Technology Officer at Makai."

Blake had all the skin-deep attributes she admired. Tall, handsome, dark complexion, deep blue eyes, muscular physique, and an enticing smile that broke into twin dimples from the corners of his kissable lips. No doubt he was a couple of years her senior. Willow had already checked out his online profile. After graduating from the Naval Academy with a degree in naval architecture, he was assigned to DARPA, the Defense Advanced Research Projects Agency, where he designed futuristic submarines, remote-controlled vehicles, and sea-floor habitats for scientific and naval intelligence missions. He earned his Masters at MIT and spent the next nine years designing fast-attack and ballistic-missile nuclear submarines.

****

Captain Hank powered up the outboard while his diminutive barefooted crewman, aptly nicknamed Shrimp, cast off the mooring lines.

"Listen up, ladies." Blake began his pre-dive briefing. "There's just the three of us so stay with me. The visibility is the best you've seen, eighty to a hundred feet. Do not, I repeat, do not go wandering off. And never swim inside the remains of this wreck. I know it's tempting, but you might get disoriented and become part of the history of this once mighty warship. Besides, the natives told me there are a few mischievous ninja spirits haunting these watery tombs."

The ladies affirmed his instructions. "Yeah, no problem," Willow said.

"Sure, we'll stick with you. You're the boss," Christy replied.

"Our maximum depth will be a hundred and ten feet, so watch your air supply. Christy, I see you have a camera. Be careful. There's much to see and photograph. I've seen some divers get distracted trying to get that perfect Nat Geo image. Check your air gauge every few breaths. Capisce?"

After squeezing into their wetsuits, they strapped on their BCs, weight belts, scuba tanks, masks, and swim fins.

"Is everyone ready?" Blake asked, grasping the front of his facemask.

Willow and Christy nodded and the three of them fell back into the tepid ocean in unison.

Blake led the ladies through the serene water to the main deck of a massive battle cruiser. Upon their arrival, he held up his right fist, a sign to hold their position for a moment while they familiarized themselves with their surroundings. Christy swam a few feet ahead and took a few pictures of Blake and Willow.

Blake then pointed his right index finger at a huge grouper standing guard over one of the decaying gun turrets. The rusting cannon was draped with ninety years of marine growth. Christy swam closer and took several more pictures of the marine life circling the giant barrel. Blake then wiggled the first two fingers of his right hand in a kicking motion, his signal for "let's go, follow me."

They inquisitively swam along the main deck while Christy continued taking photographs and making mental notes of the variety of marine life. Upon reaching the bow of the wreck, they descended another thirty feet to the sandy bottom where a pair of hundred-pound groupers had staked a claim. Knowing their bottom time was limited at a depth of one hundred and ten feet, Blake pointed to his watch and held up ten fingers indicating they would start their ascent to the surface in ten minutes.

Willow and Christy nodded and gave thumbs-up. He then pointed in the direction of the stern, and, with Blake in the lead, they commenced to swim in a single file.

After leading the women down the port side toward the stern, when he reached amidships he turned to look at the women and immediately realized that Christy was missing. He grabbed Willow by the arm to gain her attention to the situation. A wave of anguish rushed into Willow's thoughts the instant she understood Christy was no longer with them. Her eyes darted left and right searching for Christy. Bewildered and dreading the worst, she started to retrace her route, but Blake grabbed her harness and quickly checked her pressure gauge. He traced his open hand across his neck, a signal that she was low on air. He pointed both his thumbs to the surface and vigorously signaled for her to ascend. She shook her head in denial, but fearing Willow would shortly run out of air, Blake pushed her upward. Reluctantly, Willow began her ascent while Blake began searching for Christy.

Moments later, he spotted her motionless body lying on the bottom, wedged against the hull of the wreck. There were no bubbles rising from her regulator. She was not breathing.

Believing she had run out of air, Blake went into hyperdrive and instinctively executed the prescribed life-saving procedures. He took a deep breath, gripped her harness, inflated his BC, dropped his and her weight belts, and inserted his backup regulator into her mouth. After filling his lungs with air, he began to vigorously push his hand into her sternum while furiously propelling them both to the surface.

Floating face-down on the surface, Willow witnessed Blake's every lifesaving move. Upon surfacing, Shrimp and Captain Hank pulled Christy from the water. Blake promptly thrust his body into the boat and began CPR. Willow placed an oxygen mask over Christy's mouth and nose.

"She's been unconscious for about two minutes," Blake shouted.

"Come on, Christy. Come on. Breathe, breathe," Willow screamed.

Christy's lips were purple - her face as white as snow.

"I'll keep up the chest press. You hold the oxygen mask and breathe into the tube. We need to get her ventilated with oxygen."

A minute passed without any signs of recovery. The faces of Shrimp and Hank hung despondently. Blake looked at Willow, his optimism flickering.

Abruptly, Christy coughed. She coughed again and spit up a quantity of foamy sea water. She coughed again and opened her bleary eyes.

"Christy! Christy. You really gave us a scare, girl. We thought you weren't... we prayed you were going to make it." Willow gave Christy a "welcome back" stare and cupped her face between the palms of her hands.

"I'm okay," whispered Christy, pressing her hand to her forehead. "I have a terrible headache and I'm a little woozy."

"Blake saved you. You ran out of air. He found you and brought you up." Willow looked at Blake as her eyes welled up with tears. "Thank you, Blake. Thank you for saving Christy."

"It was my job."

Upon their arrival at the Chuuk docks, Christy was taken to the local hospital for observation while Willow returned to her hotel suite, took a hot shower and poured herself a glass of wine. Naked, she lay down on the bed, allowing the warm summer breeze to soothe her spirits.

She considered how impressively Blake had handled the situation. The thought of him risking his life to save her friend spawned a rush of appreciation for his courage and compassion - qualities she treasured in a man. Even though he was graying at the temples, he had the composure and strength of a Super Bowl quarterback and a profound regard for the preservation of life. That beguiling image remained in her head as she dozed off imagining what her life might become if Blake was a part of it.

It was past six and the sun was low in the horizon when she awoke. As she walked past the mirrored closet, she paused to take stock of her physical attributes. "Not too bad. Yeah, he'd like that," she muttered, putting her hands on her hips and jiggling her perky breasts. She couldn't get him out of her mind.

Unlike many women, she didn't fret over her hair, makeup, jewelry, or perfume. Never in her lifetime did she have more than a dozen pairs of shoes in her closet. Besides, she wasn't interested in a superficial or materialistic relationship. And a marriage contract with children was inconsistent with her demanding lifestyle.

"What shall I wear?" she said, pulling a pair of white shorts and a sultry red silk blouse from her closet. "These go together well - very patriotic with my strappy blue heels," she chirped. "Oh, yes, and this exquisite Ni'ihau black pupu shell necklace that Daddy gave me for earning my PhD." Setting her ensemble aside, Willow picked up her phone and dialed his room.

"Hello," Blake answered cheerfully.

"B…Blake," she stuttered. "I want to thank you again for what you did today. It was… most admirable. Listen, would you, ah, join me… for dinner. I'd really like to get to know you better. Maybe… maybe we could go for a walk on the beach."

CHAPTER 3

MUTATED TARDIGRADE

"Good morning, honey pie," Blake whispered through their open bedroom door. "How about some granola with fresh mango and pineapple? I've got breakfast waiting."

"The damn clean-up diesel woke me up. What time is it?" Willow asked, rubbing her eyes.

"Ten after eight. You can sleep in if you want. I've got to leave soon. I've got some last minute work to do on the habitat life support system before our next dive."

"No, I'll get up. I've got to get prepared for a podcast for my marine biology students. Sammy Woo and his cameraman want to shoot the entire video this coming week and I'm totally unprepared."

"What's the subject?" Blake asked as Willow sauntered into the kitchen and poured herself a cup of black Kona coffee.

"Introduction to the Great Pacific Garbage Patch."

"I hope you're not going to spoon-feed them that NOAA or UN data. We both know their numbers are pure bullshit."

"Not a chance. I've done my own research and I've got my own data. Christ, I didn't spend the past three summers on a research vessel for my health."

"You might get some flak from the university brass."

"Come on, Blake. You know I won't pull punches. It's far too critical. We're talking about what the future holds for mankind if we don't stop this mushrooming ecological crisis. And I don't think they'll fire me."

"Are you shooting the podcast in the Makai conference room?"

"Yeah, I know it's not the best audio, but I didn't want to screw around getting reservations for the university AV studio. God, everything I want to do on campus takes an act of Congress, forms, releases, prop requisitions, approvals. It's a real pain in the butt."

"No problem. Maybe we can have lunch later?"

"Okay, but I've got a lot to do to get prepared. Sammy is a demanding director. He wants to divide the podcast into three or four segments. And there are several screen- shots of maps and photos with my voice-over."

Blake read her thoughts. "I know you've got a lot on your plate. You seem frustrated. Is there a problem? You've been one of the few outspoken scientists with a conscience, righteously calling it like it is for many years."

"Almost eight years. I don't know if I've been able to make a difference," she moaned, wiping away the sleep from her eyes. "I believe the scientific community cares, but they are powerless to do anything about it. Shit, they can't even print the truth. It's all propaganda designed and approved by the oligarchs and power brokers. They control the media and precisely what the UN, NOAA, CDC, and IWC can disclose to the public. The governments and lobbyists, it's all about the money. They're not going to shut down their money-making operations just because a bunch of scientists claim the sky is falling."

She wrapped her arms around his waist and snuggled close to his chest, knowing Blake was always there for her. He was a pinnacle of strength and support, the one person she could trust to defend and protect her from this dangerous, rapidly changing world.

"So what's your next move? What do you want to do? You sound as though everything you've been telling the world is falling on deaf ears."

"I'm thinking of going into hibernation," Willow blurted. "No, I'm not resigning from my job, but maybe I should keep my mouth shut and stop preaching about the pending global disaster. Nobody is taking me seriously. There's been nothing but pushing and shoving, debate, proposals, and promises, but never any measurable action, not by us, the Japanese, the Chinese, the Russians, Europeans, Africans, Indians, or anyone. Nobody wants to invest money on solutions or follow the rules. The UN Agenda, signed by a hundred and ninety-six countries, guaranteed to clean up the oceans and restore global fisheries by 2025. It's now 2036 and the conditions are much worse. The UN Agenda was a complete disaster and so was the 2030 Global Pact on the Environment. Shit, it was nothing more than a copy of the same crap they signed twenty years earlier. They just gave it a different title. By my calculations, we've already passed the point of recovery for most of the oceanic food species. You know the whole marine biomass extinction story. We've lived with it for as long as we've been together."

Blake slowly nodded his head. "I understand, sweetheart. I really do."

Comforted by his perceptiveness, she changed the subject. "When are you mobilizing the habitat for your research dive?"

"Next Wednesday. There are four scientists, plus Doctor Joe and Davy Jones. We'll spend a couple of days briefing everyone on sea-floor habitat operations, emergency recovery, dive procedures, and decompression. Our dive site is six hundred feet deep, on the south side of Rabbit Island. It's a five-day saturation dive followed by at least six days of decompression, assuming we don't have any medical issues. I'll be at the Makai shore base until we finish decompression."

"Eleven days! How am I supposed to keep warm while you're at work? Maybe I'll join you at Makai. I know you have some extra bunks."

"Sure. I'd like that. But it won't be like the newlywed suite at the Hyatt Regency." A smile broke from the corners of Blake's lips spawning a sexy little dimple on each cheek.

"Who's on the research team? What's their specialty?"

"Bill Knight. He's the evolutionary mutations expert and the team leader. I believe you two have collaborated on other projects in the past."

"Bill and I go back a long way. He's a strong environmental advocate. He has testified before Congress and the United Nations and knows who are his friends and enemies within the international bureaucracy. We've worked on a number of projects including a six-week research trip to the garbage patch a few years ago. He's top notch, very savvy in his field. Who else?"

"Peter Zander, marine sustenance, and Walter Schmidt, an eccentric German who specializes in extremophiles, and Karen Savoy, the 'queen bee' environmental morphology expert. They're all qualified research divers so it should be a fun and rewarding trip. I believe you've met Karen before."

"Yeah, I remember Karen. Doctor Karen Savoy. What a piece of work. I wouldn't want to spend ten minutes with her at the mall. Eleven days in a cramped chamber with her would be a marathon catfight."

"Nevertheless, she's a pretty sharp scientist." Blake tried to calm her disdain.

"Let's plan a vacation when you're finished with the dive. Maybe we'll have some free time next month. Let's go to Chuuk lagoon. That's where we met and fell in love."

"As long as we're together. Hurry. Breakfast is waiting."

"Gimme a few minutes to shower and get dressed."

****

After a warm shower, Willow brushed her hair, put on her makeup and a colorful Hawaiian muumuu. Barefoot, she strolled into the kitchen and gave Blake a sloppy kiss on the lips followed by a wet-willy that quickly segued to a flirtatious tongue tracing across his ear.

"Oh, my. That was nice. Is that an invitation for an early morning rendezvous?"

"Silly man. You're not that lucky, nor that quick, and neither am I. We'll get naked tonight. I promise to be in the mood."

"I can hardly wait!" Blake gave her a wink. "Are you sure you don't want to go back to bed?"

"I'd love to. You know that. Be patient. We both know it will be well worth the wait." Willow wrapped her arms around his neck and pressed her warm body to his. "I've got to prepare my notes for the podcast. There are four hundred U of H students who are depending on me. Plus, several big box universities and public education broadcasters are interested in participating. It might just make the top ten on the national scientific podcast hit parade."

The musical ringtone of Willow's phone disrupted their playfulness.

"Hello."

"Miss Parker, this is George Hiakawa, Chief Medical Examiner for the Kauai Coroner's Office. Do you have a moment to talk?"

"Sure, George. What's on your mind?"

"There was a drowning on the island of Ni'ihau last year - a pupu shell diver named Tiki Kalani. He was free diving off the north shore and either had a heart attack or some kind of seizure. His brother and another man found his skeletal remains the next day. They placed most of it in a large plastic bag and it was ultimately delivered to my office. I attempted a standard drowning autopsy, but without the respiratory organs, I couldn't come to a definitive conclusion. The coroner ruled it an accidental drowning."

"That's very puzzling. Did you say his skeleton was discovered the following day? That doesn't make any sense."

"I think that's what his brother told the police. I don't know when he died. There was nothing left of the body except his skeleton. There was no soft tissue, cartilage, muscle or tendons connecting the bones. There was some gelatinous material covering the bones. I saved a sample of it in a cryogenic tube and stored it in liquid nitrogen at minus one-ninety-six centigrade. I never got around to conducting any further analysis. Besides, that's not my job and I really didn't know where to start. It was such an odd mystery. That's why I'm calling. I have a bad case of curiosity got the cat."

"I've never heard of a body decomposing down to the bones in such a short time. Are you sure about the time? It takes several days for marine scavengers to consume the soft tissues. Even after several weeks, there usually are a few bits and pieces of cartilage, tendons, and connective tissues."

"That's all the information I have. If you're interested I can send the sample on the next shuttle, otherwise, I'll dispose of it."

"No! I'm interested. It will make an interesting microbiological assignment for one of my students. Do you have his brother's name and phone number?"

"Yes. It's Danny Kalani, 535-1266. I'll send the sample today, air freight. You can pick it up at the airport."

"Great. I'll let you know if we find anything of value."

"Thanks, Doctor Parker. I appreciate your work. I see you on the evening news quite often."

"Thanks, George."

Willow dialed her favorite graduate student, knowing she'd be eager to earn some extra credit toward her PhD.

"Carla, this is Professor Parker. How'd you like to help me out with a special project and earn some extra credit?"

"Certainly. That would be great. What can I do?"

"I'm expecting a cryogenic package from the Kauai Coroner's Office. Can you pick it up at the Honolulu cargo terminal around one this afternoon? Then bring it to my lab here at Makai. We'll work on the project using my glove box."

"No problem. I'll see you about two."

"Who was that?" Blake inquired.

"Kauai Coroner's Office. They offered me an opportunity to analyze a sample of material they recovered from a drowning victim. Carla and I are going to do some forensic work this afternoon. It should be fun. I'll call you if I'm going to be late."

****

Carla Dixon arrived at the Makai marine biology lab at two thirty and parked her Mazda in the visitors' lot. The cryogenic storage container had been packed in a foam-lined aluminum case designed to protect the container from breakage and maintain the ultra-low temperature.

Carla was a lanky young woman from Texas, with an easy drawl and charming personality. She wore a green Hawaiian muumuu, sandals, and a ten-gallon cowboy hat allowing her long auburn hair to flow aimlessly across her tanned shoulders.

"Hey, Carla. Let me help you with that case."

"What's in this thing? Why is it so heavy?" Carla asked.

"It's filled with liquid nitrogen inside a double-walled cryogenic container. It's what's inside that interests me. Come on. Let's get this thing opened up and take a peek."

They placed the cryogenic container on a stainless steel lab table opposite a large gas-tight glove box. A pair of thick, neoprene rubber gloves hermetically sealed to the clear plastic viewing window permitted the operator to maneuver samples, tools, and testing supplies inside a Class A sterile enclosure. When pumped down to a vacuum and back-filled with nitrogen, the glove box provided an inert environment ideally suited for examining marine organisms.

Fixed between the rubber gloves was a Fisher Scientific Electron Microscope allowing the operator to safely manipulate, view and photograph microorganisms, bacteria, or potentially dangerous specimens. Two digital monitors were mounted to the top of the glove box, one for viewing the operator's hands and manipulative actions, the other displaying the magnified image of the sample as seen through the lens of the microscope.

"Okay, Carla. Let's get dressed in clean room attire, masks, and rubber gloves. We've no idea what we're dealing with so until we do, this is the prudent thing to do."

"Wow. This is really exciting. I've never done anything like this before. It's kinda spooky too."

"Watch me. You'll need to know how to do this in the real world."

Willow placed the cryogenic container inside the glove box, locked the hatch, and pumped down the internal atmosphere while flooding the interior with inert nitrogen.

"We don't want any oxygen or microbes inside the chamber that could contaminate the specimen."

With the rock-steady hands and concentration of a brain surgeon, she retrieved the sample and placed it on a stainless steel slide. Pressing a small chisel against the rock-hard frozen material, she gently tapped the top with a surgical hammer. A flake of the material dropped onto the slide.

"That was cool," Carla whispered while watching the procedure on the monitor.

"Now, let's see what we've got." Willow placed the slide on a digital scale. "Three point five grams." She then placed the slide under the microscope, set the electronic controls to one hundred magnification and fine-tuned the focus, contrast, and exposure until the most minuscule details of the image surged into view.

"Wow! Would you look at that? It looks a lot like an ice cube. You can actually see the structural formation. I'm so excited," Carla exclaimed, looking at the monitor.

"Carla, you don't need to take notes. I'll record my findings as we proceed." Willow pressed her eyes to the viewing optics. "The specimen under observation is approximately twenty millimeters square by ten millimeters thick. The material is opaque, with a single inclusion, possibly a gas pocket or a substance yet to be determined." Willow pulled back from the microscope and wiped her eyes with a tissue.

"You okay?" Carla inquired.

"Yeah, I thought I had an eyelash in my eye. I'm fine." Willow returned to the microscope.

"There appears to be an inclusion, approximately twelve millimeters long, two millimeters wide. The perimeter of the sample is beginning to melt. The melt fluid is a milky-white color similar to fat-free milk. I will conduct a chemical analysis later."

Willow jerked back from the twin viewing optics; beads of perspiration peppered her forehead. She blinked several times and wiped the sweat from her eyes while giving Carla an uneasy glance.

"Professor, are you okay? You look like you might be coming down with something."

"No, I just needed to rest my eyes for a second. I'm fine." Willow resumed her microscopic observations but immediately recoiled with a bewildered expression.

"What's the matter? You look like you just saw a ghost."

Willow began to shake. "There's something inside the sample... *and it's moving.*"

"No. No. That cannot be. Your eyes must be playing tricks on you. Nothing could live at the temperature of liquid nitrogen," Carla asserted.

"Here, you take a look." Willow stood and offered her chair to an anxious Carla.

Seconds after positioning her eyes over the optics, the adrenaline exploded into Clara's body, causing a wave of bewilderment which she overcame with a burst of curiosity and willpower.

"Fuck! What is that? It's wiggling back and forth. It looks like it is trying to free itself from the frozen material. It's got legs too, stumpy things with long, bearlike claws. Goddamit! This is bizarre, creepy, and almost supernatural. What the hell is that thing?"

"I see it on the monitor. I thought I was losing my mind. Scoot over. Let me see another close-up." Willow peered into the microscope.

"Jumpin' jellyfish! My eyes weren't playing tricks. At first, I thought it might be an ice worm, but ice worms don't have legs with claws.

"What kind of a creature is this?" Carla nervously bounced up and down on her toes.

Looking at the creature wiggling back and forth on the monitor, Willow replied. "By Golly, I think it's a water bear, a tardigrade, an extremophile."

"Tardigrade? I've read about them. Many scientists believe they came from outer space billions of years ago, buried inside an icy meteor or asteroid."

"The scientific term is called the Panspermia hypothesis. That's certainly a strong possibility. The first known tardigrade fossils are over five hundred and thirty million years old. Tardigrades are the most resilient known animals on the planet. Some species are able to survive in boiling water or the sub-zero temperatures and vacuum of deep space - places that would quickly kill any other life form except some types of bacteria or virus. They've been known to go without food or water for over a hundred years and withstand nuclear radiation levels a thousand times greater than any other organism including humans."

"What an incredible arthropod." Carla cringed and shook her shoulders.

"Yeah. But this one is completely different from any other tardigrade ever reported."

"How's that?"

"He, or she, is twelve millimeters long and much fatter. The largest known species are about half the size of a common flea. Look! It's completely free of that white material. You can see the body and head. He's translucent, difficult to see the full shape and size. But one thing is certain; this bad boy is gargantuan. Hold tight for a minute. Keep watching the monitor. I'm going to maneuver this specimen into a better position so I can get a few images of his mouth."

Willow picked up her tweezers, and with great care, positioned the head of the creature in front of the camera.

"Holy halibut! This fellow has a set of teeth that could put a bloody hole in your flesh in a matter of seconds. Carla, go into the kitchen and get me a piece of leftover meatloaf. I think it's in a plastic container on the bottom shelf."

Moments later, Carla returned with the meatloaf. Taking the tweezers, Willow pulled off a gram-size chunk of ground beef and placed it next to the tardigrade.

"What are you doing?" Carla asked.

"First, I want to see if our tardigrade likes meat. Second, and this might take a few minutes, I want to see what comes out the other end. If it matches the gelatinous white substance, we can be fairly certain this creature ate the pupu diver."

"I understand, but wouldn't it take millions of them to eat a man in one day?"

"Maybe, maybe not. If we're lucky, we can calculate a reasonable estimate of how many of these goblins it took to devour a two-hundred-pound man."

"I gotta see this."

The women watched in astonishment as the twisting creature suddenly whipped his head in the direction of the meatloaf and waddled up to his meal on his eight short legs.

"Would you look at those claws? Holy shit, he's got four or five on each foot. They look just like the claws on a grizzly bear," said Carla.

"That's how they got the nickname water bears."

"They don't look like any bear I've ever seen," snickered Carla.

"Let's see if we can estimate the volume of this creature's bite. The mouth is about a millimeter in height, width, and depth. That's one cubic millimeter in volume. A two-hundred-pound man with a thirty-six inch waist standing six feet tall would contain…" Willow paused to enter the figures into her computer. "The volume is about eight hundred thousand cubic millimeters, excluding the bones. We have to make one more assumption, that each tardi can take a bite every two seconds." Willow again paused to enter her calculations. "At that rate, each one of these meat-eaters could consume eighteen hundred cubic millimeters of human flesh per minute, without getting heartburn. A couple of thousand tardi's could theoretically devour the entire body of a big man at the rate of thirty-six thousand cubic millimeters per hour." Willow took a moment to see if Carla had fully comprehended the equation.

Carla looked up at the ceiling, her eyes dancing left to right as she processed the arithmetic. "Eight hundred thousand cubic millimeters divided by thirty-six thousand cubic millimeters per hour. *Twenty-two hours!*" Carla shouted.

"Right on, Carla."

"And all that would remain of our diver would be his bleached bones. That's rather shocking," replied Carla.

"Shocking may be too benign. It might be our worst nightmare."

"What are we going to do now?" Carla was shaking. "We've got to find a way to stop it. Or at least warn people of the danger."

"Slow down. Let's think this through. We don't know if this critter killed the diver or was just doing what scavengers do - *eat dead things*. Let's complete a genomic DNA analysis. This organism may be a new species that arrived on earth on a space rock. Or perhaps it developed from a known species via horizontal gene transfer."

"A DNA sequence? That could take several days, maybe weeks. We need to notify the authorities, the police, and the university. The public should know. This might be a life or death situation!"

"Calm down, let's use some common sense. Nobody is going to believe a couple of researchers unless we have more proof - peer-reviewed proof. What if we're wrong? What if this is just a one-off mutation? It happens in every species, humans, dogs, and cows. Did you ever see a picture of a two-headed snake?"

"But what if we're onto something big, something that could potentially kill hundreds of people?"

"You have no idea what you're talking about. If you panic, go to the press with this story, they will laugh you out of town. You'll lose your scholarship, everything you've worked toward. I'm not suggesting we keep it a secret forever. What we must do, and what we will do, is follow scientific protocol. If there's something important, a scientific discovery of a new species, one that is capable of killing and eating a human being while he or she is swimming in the ocean... well, we'd better have solid evidence to back it up. And that, Carla, means we do the genomic DNA test before even considering discussing this with anyone. Do you understand?" Willow grasped Clara by both hands and held them tightly while searching for her consensus.

"Okay."

"Promise?"

"I promise."

"Great. Now let's get to work. I'll do the basic genomic test. I should have something tomorrow, but I need to get started immediately. If that proves our hypothesis, we'll consider going public. Agreed?"

"Agreed."

"All right. I need you to complete a chemical analysis of the white matter from the meatloaf and cross-match it to the same substance in the cryogenic sample. If you get a match, we're one step closer to the solution. Don't rush, and document every step.

Pulling her cell phone from her muumuu, Willow called Blake. The fourth ring prompted the voice message request. "Blake, it's me. I'm going to be working late. The project I told you about this morning, the drowning victim, well, Carla and I are onto something that needs our immediate attention. Call me on my cell when you get a chance. Bye-bye. Love ya."

****

Although 99.9% of individual species DNA sequences are identical, enough DNA is different to distinguish a mutation of an existing organism from a different or entirely new species. The test can also determine if the subject species evolved vertically from its parents, or through horizontal gene transfer from extreme living conditions or the chemical make-up of its surrounding environment.

After gathering all the necessary chemicals, supplies, and materials needed to conduct a genomic DNA test, Willow placed the creature in a small glass test tube, added a purification solution and secured it in the centrifuge. Upon completion of the purification process, she desiccated the sample and crushed the dried body to a fine powder. Placing the powdered remains in a clean test tube, she added the appropriate amount of magnesium chloride. This procedure stabilized and amplified the DNA molecule in preparation for the DNA sequencing procedure.

While waiting for the stabilization and amplification reaction to finish, Willow returned to the lab where Carla was comparing the two white gelatinous samples for a match.

"Hey. How are you coming along?"

"I'm waiting for the enzyme response. I should have something definitive momentarily. How about you? You look beat. Nothing personal, Professor, just an observation. It's after midnight."

"I'm working on the amplification phase. I probably won't have a viable sample for several hours."

The ring of the timer told Carla her samples were ready to view. She placed the samples under the microscope and focused the images at a one hundred magnification. After a moment of eerie suspense, she turned to Willow wearing a face lined with sadness. "Take a look."

Willow's eyes snapped to attention as she viewed the images in the microscope. "Just as I thought. Both samples are fecal matter - and they match. That can only mean one thing, Carla. Our little monster ate the diver."

"I'm afraid you're right, Professor. Damn, I wish there was a way to determine if the diver was already dead... or..."

"*Eaten alive,*" Willow dolefully interrupted. "I'm going to print a hard copy of this for my files. Remember, this is our secret. I'd like you to wrap things up here and go home. Make sure you document your findings in an encrypted file before leaving."

"Professor, you're in for a long night. I'd rather stay with you. I'll keep you company."

Willow gave her a hug. "Thanks. I appreciate the company."

Carla followed Willow to her lab where the two women began to search forensic instructions for determining the time of death relative to other factors. There were several citations - death before or after burning - death before or after falling - death before or after drowning.

"I got it," Willow blurted as she read the introduction out loud. "Determining the cause of death before or after a drowning is one of the most difficult challenges for a forensic pathologist, particularly if there are no wounds, signs of a struggle, or an eyewitness. In rare cases, where the victim is murdered in fresh water then dumped into a lake or the ocean, the pathologist can extract water from the lungs. If the body was recovered from the ocean, but the lungs are filled with fresh water, it was probably murder. Huh. Shit, that's worthless information." Willow was frustrated.

After several hours of research without a sliver of useful information, Willow was about to give up when she recalled something the Chief Medical Examiner had told her.

"Wait!" she launched off her chair. "We might have a witness."

It was six in the morning when she dialed the number.

"Hello," answered a groggy male.

"Danny. Is this Danny Kalani?"

"Yes. Why are you calling me at this hour? You woke me up."

"I'm professor Willow Parker. I work for the University of Hawaii and Makai Institute of Marine Technology in Waimanalo. I'm doing some forensic work trying to determine the cause of your brother's death."

"That was a year ago. The case is closed. The cops didn't do a goddamn thing. They said it was an accident. I didn't believe them then, and I still don't."

"I'm onto something, a clue. It may not pan out but I need to ask you a couple of questions. Okay?"

"Go on."

"I understand you and a friend found his body. Can you tell me how you found him?"

"The back of his skull, that's what I saw first - the back of his skull. There was no hair. Tiki had long hair. He kept it in a ponytail when he was free diving for shells. His head was upright, on top of the sand, on the white sand next to a wall of lava. His arms, or what was left of them, were spread out like an eagle on top of the sand. The rest of him was buried several feet into the sand. It was a horrible sight. I still have nightmares."

"I'm so sorry. Was there any sign of a weapon, or a struggle?"

"No. But we had a tough time retrieving his remains. He… I mean his skeleton was upright, like a mannequin. Only his skull and arms were above the bottom. Everything else was buried in some kind of gooey white material. It was all over the bottom. All we got back… was…" Danny began to cough… "his bones." Danny lost control of his emotions and began to sob. "I'm sorry. I can't erase the image of his skull, my dear brother's head, sticking out of the sand."

"That is most puzzling. What was he wearing?"

"A facemask, swimsuit, and a nylon belt. His expensive watch was wrapped around his wrist. His black pupu shell lei was still around his neck."

"Was he happy? Did he show any signs of depression, financial problems, or relationship issues?"

"Hell, no," Danny indignantly insisted. "Tiki was a professional pupu free diver. Everyone loved him. He was planning to get married."

"I'm sorry. I didn't mean to upset you. I'm just trying to get a more complete picture of what happened. Did the police question you or anyone else you know?"

"Negative. The coroner declared it an accidental drowning. But I believe something is wrong - the pieces don't fit. Tiki called me about six. Said he had some problems with a fishing net and would not be able to come to my house for a BBQ. I believe he was going to spend some time shell diving before sundown and crash at my place. I sure hope you can put the puzzle together. It would mean a lot to our family and his fiancée."

"One last question, please. What time was it when you found him?"

"About four in the afternoon."

"Thanks, Danny. Call me if you think of anything else." Willow terminated the call and scratched her head.

"Was that helpful?" Carla asked.

"It answers the questions about where and when he died."

"And?"

"He died while free diving for shells off Keawanui beach between six in the evening and four o'clock the following afternoon."

"Wait, that doesn't leave much time for some minuscule creatures to devour his flesh down to the bone."

"No, it doesn't. That is increasingly difficult for me to comprehend," Willow said, ruffling her hair with both hands.

"What shall we do now?" Carla asked.

"I've got to complete my genomic DNA test."

****

Carla closely followed Willow down the hall to the DNA laboratory. They passed through the airlock, wiggled into sterile white coveralls, placed a surgical mask over their nose and mouth and stabbed their hands into skin-tight surgical gloves. Passing into the lab, the misty antiseptic atmosphere foreshadowed their intentions.

Willow opened the cover, retrieving the amplified sample. Holding the glass test tube firmly, she added a few milliliters of ethidium bromide for staining the DNA, slipping between the nucleotides that make up a DNA double helix.

"This process is known as intercalation," Willow said to her inquisitive co-conspirator. "Once I place this sample in the sequencer, it will be illuminated with a UV source, binding the ethidium bromide to the sample. The computer will then sequence the DNA to determine the genomic markers and compare it to our database of known organisms."

"This is fascinating. But I'm a little nervous," Carla confessed. "How long do we have to wait for the results?"

"Just a few minutes."

"How exactly does PCR analysis work? You can give me the scientific description. I've got to learn to speak the proper terminology."

"Polymerase chain reaction or PCR analysis mimics the biological process of DNA replication but confines it to specific DNA sequences. The sample is first purified and then denatured into the separate individual polynucleotide strains by heating. PCR uses replication enzymes that are tolerant of high temperatures. With this process, additional copies of the sequence are generated - the more, the better. The computer does all the heavy lifting including UV illumination, DNA sequencing, and comparing the sample to a database containing DNA signatures from over a million organisms. It's kinda like the FBI fingerprint database used to identify the bad guys. It may sound complicated, but after you do it a few times, it's like putting on your makeup."

"Aren't you nervous about the results? I am."

"Of course I am. But it's more than that. Besides being antsy, even scared, I'm angry - mad as hell at the human race for their disregard for Mother Nature. We may be the most intelligent animals on the planet, but that doesn't necessarily equate to making good choices. We have the dubious reputation for being the deadliest species on the planet."

Willow's rant was interrupted by the ding-ding ring of the computer. Her eyes opened wide like a deer staring down the lights of an approaching car.

"It's… time." Willow waited impatiently for the printout.

Moments later, she tore the long strip of paper from the computer. While holding one end in her right hand, her left hand slid along the edge, stopping from time to time to confirm specific data points. Halfway down the list was an asterisk. Next to it was the genomic name of the sample and a footnote.

"*Hypsibius dujardini*. Tardigrades," Willow cried out. "No, no, no. That can't be."

Willow began to tremble while continuing to scan the printout, hoping to find some contravening data. "Yelping yellowtail!" Willow exclaimed. "It's definitely a match. Wait, there's a footnote. It says the DNA marker for horizontal gene transfer was *twenty-seven percent.*"

"Is that good or bad?" Carla asked.

"I'm afraid it's very bad. Actually, it's much worse than that. Tardigrades are one of the few examples of an extremophile. They live in all the oceans and seas of the world. They are carnivorous. Whoops, I almost missed it. There's another footnote. It says trace amounts of PCBs and polystyrene derivatives were identified. This footnote means our little monster has genetically mutated due to environmental changes."

"So why are you trembling?"

"Tardigrades don't have teeth. They have a small mouth and a stylet for chewing microscopic organisms. This is definitely a mutation, probably due to the toxic effects of photodegradation of the plastics floating in the Great Pacific Garbage Patch."

"Holy shit!"

"And the predecessor of this creature is only a millimeter long. Our sample is twelve millimeters. Come with me. I'll show you an image taken twenty years ago." Willow led Carla to another computer where she logged on and quickly opened the appropriate file. Leaning back in her chair, she waited for the image to appear on the screen.

"Come on, come on," Willow muttered, waving her hand in a beckoning motion.

The image locked onto the screen. Willow thrust her index finger at it and shouted, "That's a tardigrade. It's no larger than a flea. See, it has a small circular mouth and looks like an uncircumcised penis." Willow and Carla snickered together.

"Too small," Carla giggled.

"We shouldn't be laughing. I'd better print this image so we have hard copies of both tardigrades - twenty years apart."

April 2015: Pacific Tardigrade: (Hypsibius dujardinis)

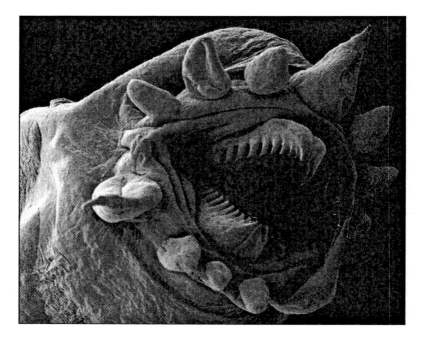

June 2036: Pacific Tardigrade: (Hypsibius dujardinis)

CHAPTER 4

DANCE OF THE HAGFISH

"Welcome to the Makai Institute of Marine Technology. For those of you who don't know me, my name is Blake Reynolds. I'm the Chief Technology Officer and Director of this saturation diving operation. This handsome gentleman to my right is Maxie O'Donnell. Maxie is captain of the *Kanaloa,* the Ruler of the Sea. She's our habitat support vessel. The man to my left is Dr. Joseph McMasters. Doctor Joe is a renowned hyperbaric physician, cinematographer, and notorious explorer. He will join you during the saturation diving and decompression operations. Next to him is David Jones. Davy is your Diving Supervisor." Everyone shook hands with a congenial greeting. "Everyone, please follow me for a tour of our mobile undersea habitat, *Welina.* That's Hawaiian for an affectionate greeting."

The scientists shuffled from one foot to the other, eager to see a tour of what would soon be their home on the bottom of the ocean.

As they walked down the Makai pier to the habitat, Bill Knight offered Blake some background on the other scientists. "Pete and Walt are experienced divers but have never been under saturation conditions deeper than two hundred feet. I don't think it will be a problem, but I thought you should know."

"I've read their resumes. They've passed the physical. Two hundred feet or six hundred feet, if they follow the rules they'll be fine. If not, the deeper depth probably won't make much of a difference."

"You're probably right. Anyway, I know they're a bit antsy. Who wouldn't be? They'll be spending five days at six hundred feet in near-freezing water followed by six more days inside a cramped steel cylinder. For my money, that's much more hazardous than riding a computer-controlled spaceship to the backside of the moon."

"They'll be okay. Davy won't let them do anything stupid. What about Karen Savoy?"

"She's got more diving experience than most of us. However, she has garnered a reputation as a prima donna. She can be quite demanding. But she knows her subject matter and will complement our work."

Moored to the pier, the bright yellow habitat vacillated ever so gently in the Makai boat basin.

"Here she is, folks, all five hundred tons and your future underwater home for an all-expenses-paid vacation to the bottom of the Pacific Ocean."

"Wow! She's one beautiful machine. She's huge. I'm blown away." Pete shook his head in wonderment, trying to grasp how much engineering expertise and money this masterpiece required. The scientists had seen pictures of the habitat, but the sheer size of her floating in the Makai boat basin was overwhelming.

"First, let me point out a few important features. *Welina* operates like a twin-hulled submarine without any engines. The habitat is firmly attached to the hydrodynamic catamaran hull and can easily be towed to the dive site by *Kanaloa*. Except for electrical power from *Kanaloa,* she is entirely autonomous. Everything you'll need is provided - mixed gas, warm bunks, communications, power, food, water, medical supplies, and a space-rated life support system. The large chambers amidships are the living, diving, and laboratory compartments. There's room for six, so you'll have plenty of space. Those elongated steel tubes on either side are filled with high-pressure, helium-oxygen breathing gas - enough to pressurize the habitat and support your diving needs for the duration of your mission. Outboard of the gas tubes are high-pressure air tanks for blowing ballast to return to the surface. Those capsules on each end are emergency escape modules. When released, they float to the surface. We tow them back to the Makai pier for decompression."

"Where is the dive site?" Pete asked, looking out to sea.

"Out there." Blake extended his arm and pointed his index finger. "Just to the left of Rabbit Island, about five miles from where we're standing. It takes about an hour for *Kanaloa* to get there while towing the habitat."

Blake scanned the faces of the four scientists looking for signs of trepidation or angst. "Let's check out the interior. Watch your step. We'll enter through the main hatchway in the center of the habitat."

Everyone cautiously shuffled their way across the grated metal gangway to the main hatchway, where they climbed down a set of steel rungs into the diving chamber. Here, in the confines of the ten-foot-diameter spherical chamber, they formed a tight circle. If anyone had any predisposition to claustrophobia, this is where it might appear.

Blake continued describing the habitat. "The interior of the diving chamber was painted with pure white marine-grade enamel specially formulated to resist bacteria and mold growth - two of the most troublesome ailments saturation divers' experience. Two UV-C lamps also inhibit the growth of mold. If for some reason you experience ear pain, see Doctor Joe immediately. He'll give you some magical sauce that will take care of it."

Peter was curious to learn more about the operating procedures. "I know Davy is in charge of the ballast control system, but with so many different valves, gauges, tubes, and pipes, it's hard to comprehend how this jig-saw puzzle works. Please give us a quick summary of what all this plumbing is designed to do?"

"It's quite simple. The small diameter plumbing is for pressurizing the dive equipment and to control the flow and pressure of the habitat life support system. The large diameter system controls the flooding and venting of the ballast tanks. The interior of the diving chamber is appointed with accessories that make diving operations run efficiently. Along one quadrant are two fold-down, reinforced fiberglass chairs. These are reserved for the divers while they dress out in their dry suits and diving apparatus. Lockers are available for you to store your personal items, dry suit, undergarments, fins, towels, and dry clothing.

"You'll be diving with the most advanced closed-circuit oxy-helium dive rigs with full facemasks. A solid-state diver communication system is integrated into your facemasks. These rigs have been upgraded with the latest helium voice unscrambler. When you talk, you won't sound as much like Donald Duck as you would without it. Primary communication between *Welina* and *Kanaloa* is via a fiber optic cable, with a wireless blue-green laser as back-up. You've all used these before, right?"

Blake received a verbal affirmation or a nod from each scientist.

"I'm also pleased to announce that we've provided everyone with a commemorative titanium dive knife, laser inscribed with your name and the date of your momentous dive. Davy Jones will hand these out before we commence operations. Any questions?"

"Who's in charge of the ballast controls and communications?" Pete asked.

"Davy will operate the ballast controls and communications. Doctor Joe will manage the diving operations and life support systems. Once you lock-out, you're pretty much on your own. Just remember to follow the proper dive and safety protocols you've been trained to use."

"Where do we get some zzzs?" asked Walter.

"Follow me to the living quarters. Watch your heads going through this passageway."

Traveling in a single line, the dive team followed Blake into the living chamber and gathered around the perimeter.

"Whoa! This place is huge. Much bigger than I expected," Peter exclaimed.

"It's the largest undersea habitat ever built," Bill replied.

Blake kept the conversation moving forward. "The living and working chambers are sized to meet NASA space travel recommendations - five hundred cubic feet per person for missions of thirty days or less."

"Pick a bunk. Ladies first." Blake smiled at Karen. "Davy and Doctor Joe will sleep in the top bunks. The head and shower are at the far end." Blake pointed to the narrow door similar to a commercial airliner. "Is everyone familiar with the shower rules? We have a limited supply of fresh water so you'll be limited to a single two-minute shower per day."

"Hey, what about me. I've got to shampoo my hair. You don't expect me to run around looking like some street hooker," Karen barked. "Besides, I've got more hair than all you guys combined," she sneered. It was apparent Karen had no desire to improve her well-deserved bitchy reputation.

Bill shrugged her comment aside but gave her no satisfaction. "I understand some of you may be a bit nervous about this deep dive. But we're all in this together." Bill gave Karen a fatherly glance. "You also signed a contract. I'm sure Walter would be happy to give anyone a free haircut before the dive." Everyone snickered except Karen.

"Jesus, can't a girl get a little respect."

"What about waste? This place is going to get pretty ripe," Walt asked.

Blake understood everyone's concern for good housekeeping. "There's a waste disposal lock by the head. Walter, I'm putting you in charge. Every bit of garbage, including you-know-what, will be locked out of the habitat daily. It will be stored in an exterior holding tank and properly disposed of after the dive. Everyone knows the personal hygiene protocol. Please stick to it." A few scrutinizing eyes drifted toward Karen.

"What?" Karen shrugged her shoulders.

"Now follow me into the laboratory. Watch your head as we move through the hatchways." Everyone followed Blake to the laboratory.

"Here's where you'll conduct your work. This lab is equipped with everything you asked us to provide. There are microscopes, slide preparation and preservation materials, centrifuge, and a liquid nitrogen cryogenic storage container. All the necessary instruments are in these two metal cabinets. At the far end is where Doctor Joe keeps his medical supplies. There are two high-speed computers, a compact DNA sequencer, and an Internet hot spot. I assume you each brought your laptop or tablet."

Welina seafloor habitat at Makai harbor

The following morning, Bill Knight stood at the whiteboard watching his dive team nervously sipping their morning cup of Kona coffee. Doctor Joe and Davy Jones sat in the back of the conference room, reviewing dive schedules, safety, communications, and emergency procedures while Maxie completed a final inspection of *Kanaloa* and the tow lines to the habitat.

"Let's get started, shall we. This won't take long," Bill said, waving his clipboard. "You've each been given a binder with all the details of our saturation dive. The purpose of this mission is to determine if the increased levels of plastic photodegradation in the Great Pacific Garbage Patch has resulted in any changes in the food preferences or other characteristics of the marine organisms that populate this part of the ocean. Our first task is to stake out a test grid a few yards from the habitat. Nylon grid lines need to be secured with stainless steel spikes. These grid lines will divide the test area into sixteen separate feeding zones - each four meters square. Half of the feeding zones will be baited for carnivores, the other half with various algae and seaweeds for herbivores. Karen, you and Walter will stake out the carnivorous quadrants. Peter and I will do likewise for the herbivores."

"What's the bait?" Karen interrupted.

"Sardines, squid, bay shrimp, krill, periwinkles, fan coral, sea cucumbers, and crab."

"Why not billfish, tuna, or sharks? They represent a large portion of all fish in the sea. And it's a big sea, almost four hundred thousand square miles," Karen asked in a self-aggrandizing tone, searching the faces of her fellow divers for consensus.

"I believe those species are on the list of endangered species." Bill was more informed than Karen and was determined to not let her dictate the mission plan.

"Just asking," Karen meekly replied, knowing she'd been outgunned.

Bill continued the briefing, answered a few more questions and finally checked his dive watch. "Okay, let's board the habitat and secure our personal gear. We'll have lunch on the *Kanaloa* while underway to the dive site."

****

After securing their personal equipment, the dive team took up their assigned positions for the descent to the bottom. Everyone wore blue coveralls over thermal underwear. A pale red, white, and blue shoulder patch was stitched to the right shoulder containing an American flag surrounded by gold lettering that read, *Makai Institute of Marine Technology.*

While the habitat remained on the surface, the dive team simmered from the Hawaiian heat. Once the habitat was on the bottom, the internal temperature of the habitat would be near freezing. Furthermore, the poor thermal properties of the helium-rich breathing atmosphere produced a chill factor several degrees colder than the water temperature.

In preparation for the descent, the divers positioned themselves a few feet apart, from one end of the habitat to the other. Bill Knight joined Davy and Doctor Joe in the dive chamber. Peter Zander and Walter Schmidt sat in the lab area. Karen Savoy sat on her bunk in the living quarters.

"This is *Kanaloa*," Maxie called on the comm line. "How do you read me, over?"

"Five by five. Signal strength and comprehension are good," Davy replied. "We're ready to proceed with the pre-dive checklist, over."

"Roger. What is your helium pressure, over?" Maxie asked.

"Helium gas pressure is forty-five hundred psi," replied Davy.

"Roger. What is your air pressure, over?"

"Air pressure is forty-two hundred and fifty psi."

"Scrubber efficiency for each chamber, over?"

"Living quarters ninety-eight. Diving chamber ninety-nine. Working area ninety-six. All systems go, over?"

"Battery amp/hours, over."

"Twenty-five hundred, over."

"Pressure check, over."

Davy opened the helium supply valve increasing the internal habitat pressure by one pound per square inch. "Pressure test complete. We're tight, over."

"It's now 1310 hours. You may commence pressurized descent at will, over."

"Roger. We're commencing pressurized descent. Setting lapsed runtime to zero-zero, over."

"Roger. Lapsed run time set to zero-zero."

"Attention all personnel," Davy spoke with an imposing tone. "We are about to commence our descent," he shouted. "Please make sure you equalize your ears at the onset of pressurization. There are internal pressure gauges mounted to the bulkheads of every compartment. Everyone, please sound off when I call out your name. Doctor Joe."

"Go."

"Bill."

"Go."

"Peter."

"Go."

"Walt."

"Ya."

"Karen."

"I'm always ready."

With the twist of his wrist, Davy opened the main helium supply valve allowing high-pressure helium gas to flood into the habitat with a deafening, high-pitched roar. Doctor Joe took a few seconds to equalize and then ducked through the hatchway into the laboratory chamber to check on Peter and Walter.

"Fifty feet, sixty feet, seventy feet." Davy counted down the depth over the intercom.

The roar of the helium gradually segued into a high-frequency whistle. The sweet smell of helium raced through everyone's nostrils.

"Two hundred feet. Two ten. Two twenty. All systems go."

The habitat suddenly shook like a minor earthquake.

"What the fuck was that?" Karen squealed.

"Thermocline. Just a thermocline," Bill reassured her.

"Four hundred. Four twenty."

"Five hundred feet. Prepare for landing." Davy warned.

"Five fifty. Five sixty. Five seventy. Five eighty." Everyone clutched the most convenient grip. "Five ninety."

The bow struck first, sending a frightening shockwave throughout the hull like a single beat from a giant kettledrum. Moments later, the stern made contact with the sandy bottom with a dull swooshing sound.

"Depth, six-zero-five bow to stern. We're home and on the level," Davy shouted.

After a round of high-fives and hooyah's, the dive team settled down to business. Bill called for a pre-dive briefing to review the first dive plan and safety procedures. Davy Jones and Doctor Joe joined the team in the living chamber.

"Karen, you and Walt will be the first pair to lock-out. Your job is to set the grid lines and secure the carnivore baits according to the sketch in your binder. Your allotted bottom time is sixty minutes. You've rehearsed this procedure several times so there is no need to rush."

Karen interrupted. "Yeah, Walter. Take your time, but don't slow me down."

"Let me remind everyone to stay close to your dive buddy. That goes for you too, Karen. Don't overwork your breathing apparatus and most importantly, check in with Davy every five minutes. There's plenty of underwater lighting, so your task should not be difficult. If there are no questions, Karen, you and Walt can get suited up."

Upon entering the lock-out chamber, Karen immodestly stripped down to her underwear in view of Walt and Davy. She then slipped into her woolen undergarment, wiggling her fanny provocatively. Looking like a centerfold, fuzzy-wuzzy teddy bear, she inched into her dry suit.

"Walter, would you be a dear and zip me up," Karen cooed, turning her backside to Walter.

Without a word, Walter pulled the water-tight zipper across her shoulders and locked it into place.

Davy helped Walt with his dry suit and assisted both divers with their diving equipment.

"Com check, Walter."

"Five by five. Good to go."

"Com check, Karen."

"No problem. Let's go."

"Divers enter the water," Davy said, making note of their start time in his dive log.

Karen put on her fins and climbed down the ramp leading to the water, carrying a canvas bag of specially prepared baits. When she reached the next-to-last step, rather than easing her body into the water, she jumped. As she fell forward, the leg of her dry suit snagged the corner of the ladder, tearing a three-inch-long hole in the left ankle of her dry suit. "Fuck!' Karen yelled. "I've got a hole in my suit. Goddamn it. Whoever designed this dive ladder should be tarred and feathered."

"Karen, do you want to abort?" Davy asked.

"Not a chance. It's just a small tear. I'll take on some water but I won't drown."

"Are you hurt or bleeding?"

"Yeah, just a little. Don't worry. It's just a scratch. I'll be fine. Tell Walter to get his ass in the water. We're wasting time and I'm short on patience."

Walter followed, holding a reel of nylon rope in one hand, with the strap of a canvas bag containing a dozen foot-long anchor pins and a ball-peen hammer slung over his shoulder.

The water temperature hovered around thirty-eight degrees. Visibility with the exterior lights was fifty feet. Strangely, there wasn't a single fish, crab, or any other signs of marine life.

Walter swam a few yards and stopped to set the first of his anchor pins. Karen had distanced herself and began to place her baits every few feet along the bottom.

"Karen. Wait up. I need you to pull the rope tight while I set the anchor pins," Walt complained.

"Jesus, do I have to do everything."

Walter drove in the first anchor pin and secured the bitter end of the rope while Karen swam in the opposite direction.

Walter then swam to the next anchor point and drove another pin into the sand.

In spite of Karen's shenanigans, they managed to install all the grid lines in thirty minutes.

"Karen, your baits are not evenly spaced inside the grid lines," Walt protested.

"Don't tell me what to do," Karen snapped.

"Hey, look, there's a hagfish. I guess he smelled your bait. Here comes another. Davy, are you seeing these hagfish on the monitor?"

"Yeah, I got em. Looks like a few more are coming for the bait."

Paying no heed to the hagfish, Karen and Walt began to reposition the baits.

"Karen, your dry suit has a tear at the ankle and you're bleeding."

"I know. My suit is flooded up to my knees. Hurry up. I need to get back to the habitat. I'm starting to shiver."

"Here come more hagfish. Christ Almighty, I've never seen so many. They're eating all the bait."

"Ouch! Fuck!" Karen screamed, frantically smacking her legs like a frustrated tennis pro smashing his racket after double-faulting match point. "There's a fucking hagfish inside my suit," Karen shrieked. "Owee! He's biting my legs. It hurts really bad. I'm bleeding everywhere! Oh, God. Now there are two of them. Owee! Help me, Walter! Help! Owee! Yeeaowee!"

"Karen, what's wrong?" Davy hollered.

The only response was a train of horrific screams.

"Walter, what's happening to Karen?" Davy yelled.

"Hagfish! Lots of them. They got inside her dry suit. There's blood everywhere. There's more, all fighting to get inside her suit. They're ejecting slime everywhere. Oh, God. This is unbelievable!"

"Get her back to the habitat," Davy shouted while looking at the carnage on the video monitor.

Walt had a close-up view of the situation and justly feared for his life. For a brief moment he thought he might be able to save her, but more hagfish appeared and he lost his mettle.

Soon, countless numbers of foot-long carnivores were frantically competing for their share of Karen's warm flesh - their snake-like bodies squirming up her legs to the most private parts of her body, spinning and twirling, probing and biting, tearing off pieces of flesh as they moved up her thighs toward her abdominal cavity.

"Walter, are you able to get to Karen?" Davy bellowed.

"Negative. I'm not going anywhere near her. It's a bloodbath. These creatures are man-eaters - not like any hagfish I've seen or heard of before."

Walter raced back to the habitat and launched himself up the ladder into the dive chamber. Ripping off his facemask, he looked at Davy and Doctor Joe with shell-shocked eyes shrouded by a terror-stricken, white-washed face.

Suddenly, Karen stopped fighting and her arms drifted aimlessly at her side.

Everyone in the dive chamber saw the carnage on the monitor.

"She's gone," Doctor Joe declared, bowing his head in reverence. "I think we need to figure out how to handle the body, or what's left of it," Doctor Joe muttered with the dignity and compassion of his professional doctrine.

Dazed, Davy continued to watch the butchery as more and more hagfish wiggled their way into the feeding frenzy.

"There's not going to be much left of her to recover." Davy turned away and vomited.

"Shut that monitor down!" Doctor Joe commanded. "It's too morbid. We've got to figure out a way to retrieve her body," he said, wiping the sweat from his eyes. "We need to get a rope on her before a shark takes her."

"Davy, how about the RCV?"

"Negative. It's not configured for knot tying."

Doctor Joe looked for a volunteer. "Walt?"

"No fucking way," Walt bellowed, vigorously shaking his head.

Exhausted from the dispiriting drama they had witnessed, everyone joined Doctor Joe in the living quarters to mourn the loss of one of their own.

****

With the exterior monitor down and the crew emotionally played out, nobody saw or recorded the shimmering, translucent cloud gracefully emerge from the dark dystopia of the surrounding sea.

Like a cumulus cloud, the hippo-sized mass drifted toward the habitat, shape-shifting its cloudlike bulk as it advanced a few feet above the seabed. As the mass approached the corpse, it gave birth to hundreds of miniature cyclones - each one containing a colony of half-inch-long, translucent organisms.

While they swirled, the colonies emitted random pulses of iridescent blue-green light, communicating information from one colony to another. Each colony moved in unison with the others until the mass completely shrouded Karen's corpse.

As if on command from a higher authority, the churning cloud of organisms rushed into the opening of Karen's dry suit, like water spiraling down the drain.

Moments later, there was a tumultuous upheaval of activity inside Karen's dry suit - like a sack of ravenous rats, undulating, fighting, pushing, biting, desperately trying to escape.

First, there was one, quickly followed by a pair. Then, in a frantic exodus, the entire lot of brownish-purple hagfish dashed from the confines of Karen's dry suit and disappeared into the darkness, leaving a trail of slimy mucus in their wake.

****

"What are you doing?" Davy inquired as Doctor Joe slipped into his dive gear.

"It's been four hours. I'm going to check on Karen," Doctor Joe replied. "Turn on the external camera. And be sure to warn me if you see any hagfish."

"Shit, Joe, you must be nuts. What's that bottle you're carrying?"

"Preservative - the kind we use to store marine organisms for future analysis. I'm going to stick this tube inside her dry suit and empty the contents. If there are still any hagfish inside her suit, maybe this will force them to leave."

"Brilliant! But are you sure you want to go out there?" Davy asked.

"No. In fact, I'm scared as hell. But someone has to do it. We can't leave her body out there."

"I'll watch the monitor and let you know if I see any hagfish or sharks. You'd better get your ass back here immediately."

Doctor Joe exited the habitat, approached Karen's body and then gently ran his hand over her dry suit feeling for any signs of hagfish.

"Davy, I don't feel anything moving. Maybe the hagfish left. Just in case, I'm enlarging the tear in her dry suit to make it easier for them to escape the same way they entered. Goddamit! Yuk. Her suit is filled with hagfish slime. They must have been pretty stressed out to leave so much of it inside her suit." Doctor Joe pulled his fingers through the sand removing some of the viscous liquid.

"Sorry about the slime. It's a defense mechanism. When stressed, they squirt mucus from glands running the length of their body. The mucus turns to slime and expands twenty times its original volume when exposed to seawater. It's the perfect getaway from a dangerous predator," Davy said.

"Thanks for the science lesson," replied Doctor Joe as he maneuvered toward her facemask.

Lurching back in repugnance, he screamed. "Holy shit. There's nothing left of her - nothing but bones. Not an ounce of soft tissue. They ate her eyes and hair too. Her skull is all that is left of her head."

"Calm down, Doc. You don't want to overwork your gear. Take a few deep breaths and stay cool," Davy warned.

"There's something terribly wrong. Hagfish didn't do this. Their mouths are too big and their teeth are more like fingernails. Something else has been here." He rolled the corpse over and unzipped her dry suit, exposing the skeletal remains of her upper torso.

"Davy, the hagfish are gone, but there are a few bits and pieces. Wait, we might have another intruder. I'm holding one on the tip of my finger. It's some kind of worm, about a half inch long. I found a few more. If I had to guess, I'd bet this organism joined in the feeding frenzy. Man, this is some eerie sight. I'll bring back a few samples for Bill. Maybe he can figure out what they are."

****

"*Welina*, this is Doctor Joe. Over."

"Hi, Doc. Thanks for calling. What's up?" Captain Maxie asked.

"Karen is dead."

"What the fuck! What happened?" Maxie bellowed.

"We don't have all the facts. It looks like she was attacked by a school of hagfish and perhaps some other kind of organism. She accidentally tore her dry suit and there was blood in the water. Maybe that's what attracted the hagfish. They got inside her suit through the tear. Later, some other organism got inside too. They… consumed…" Doctor Joe stuttered. "They consumed her flesh. There's nothing left but her bones."

"Holy hell. How…what… why?"

"I can't explain it. Something is terribly wrong. I've never seen anything like this before."

"Did you say there was nothing left but her skeleton?"

"Affirmative. I'm going to put her remains in one of the escape capsules and send her body to the surface. Call the Coast Guard and coroner's office and have them take possession of her body. Frankly, none of us want it to remain inside the habitat. And contact Blake. He needs to get involved."

"Yeah, I understand. I'll let Blake know what's happened and get back to you."

****

With the Coast Guard vessel standing by topside, Doctor Joe and Walt locked out of the habitat and swam toward Karen's remains. Doctor Joe removed her diving rig and weight belt, zipped up her dry suit to preserve and protect what was left of the attack, and secured a towel across her facemask. Walter took a grip on her legs while Doctor Joe inflated her BC to make her body neutrally buoyant. The two men then maneuvered her body to the lower entrance hatch of one of the escape capsules.

"Hold it for a moment while I rig the block and tackle," Doctor Joe said while opening the bottom hatch.

Hanging from the capsule ceiling was a four-part block and tackle and a special harness designed to permit one diver to lift an incapacitated diver through the narrow hatchway and into the capsule.

"Okay, Walt. Secure her to the harness. I'll pull her into the capsule while you help navigate her body through the hatchway."

"I got it," Walt replied. "Give me a minute to secure the harness." Walt wrapped the harness around the body and tightened the straps. "Okay. Ready when you are."

From inside the capsule, Doctor Joe pulled on the block and tackle rope while Walt guided Karen's remains through the hatchway.

"We're done here," Doctor Joe said as he exited the capsule. "I've dogged the inner hatch and checked the pressure. The capsule is tight. Give me a hand closing the outer hatch and we'll head back to the habitat."

"God, that was one of the most emotional experiences of my life. I never want to do that again." Walt struggled to control his emotions.

"Davy, this is Doctor Joe. We're finished here. You can release the capsule. Let Maxie know the capsule is on its way to the surface."

****.

"*Welina,* this is Blake. Come back."

"Blake, this is Doctor Joe. I assume Maxie gave you the gory details?"

"Yes, he did. What an outrageous experience for everyone, it was very grotesque and freaky. How is everyone holding up?"

"As you would expect, shaken and scared. They're thankful that whatever it was that attacked Karen didn't do the same to them. There's lots of scientific talk about how and why this happened. And everyone is concerned this gruesome event may not be the last. Bill plans to conduct some DNA work during decompression. Maybe we'll know more in a few days."

"I spoke with Karen's parents. Naturally, they were devastated, but after a while, we were able to talk rationally. I explained the situation and told them how difficult it was to bring her body back from a deep dive. They were grateful for how we handled the situation and understood that five other lives were at stake. They insisted we bring her back, so your idea of using one of the escape capsules was a good one. Did you get a chance to conduct an autopsy?"

"Not really. The official autopsy and certificate of death must be issued by the coroner. I looked at the physical evidence. It was… how can I put it… a terrifying death. I'm reasonably certain she died from a loss of blood shortly after the hagfish attacked. I think she bled out. But the strangest thing was the hagfish suddenly disappeared or were driven out, possibly by a different marine creature. It looks like a maggot or a small worm of some type. I was able to grab a few of them, plus a few bits of hagfish including a partly eaten head for Bill to examine later. Bill thinks these wormlike creatures ate everything that was left by the hagfish. We've got some video. It's really gruesome."

"I told Maxie to bring you guys home. He's ready to tow you back to Makai for decompression as soon as you surface. Go ahead and wrap things up and make the habitat ready to surface. You know the drill. Button down all the hatches, make sure *Welina* is gas-tight. Let Maxie know when you leave the bottom. You'll be on the surface within minutes."

CHAPTER 5

THE GREAT PACIFIC GARBAGE PATCH

"Doctor Parker, we're ready to tape your podcast." Sammy Woo said while fine-tuning the focus on his video camera. "Please look into the camera while you speak. If you need to pause or take a break, just raise your hand. If you lose your place or need a drink of water we can edit it out and retake. Are you ready?"

"Let's go," Willow replied as she ignited her game face.

Willow had dressed in a modest black business skirt with a long-sleeved white silk blouse and dressy black pumps. Her long blond hair hung down to her shoulders, partially hiding the black pupu shell lei encircling her neck. This wasn't her first podcast. In fact, she led the university in podcast productions while earning numerous accolades from her superiors, colleagues, and students. However, she always felt as though she could have been better prepared.

Sammy stepped in front of Willow with the clapperboard facing the camera. "Doctor Willow Parker podcast, take one."

"Good morning. I'm Willow Parker, Dean of the Marine Biology department at the University of Hawaii. Welcome to this podcast entitled 'The Great Pacific Garbage Patch.' After the podcast, those of you who have registered will receive a password to access the exam. You may email questions to the address shown on the screen."

Willow cleared her throat and took a drink of water.

"In 1988, the Great Pacific Garbage Patch, also known as the Pacific trash vortex, was first described by NOAA, the National Oceanic and Atmospheric Administration. Their report was based on the results of several research studies measuring plastic debris in the North Pacific Ocean."

A map of the North Pacific Ocean appeared on the four large monitors hanging from each of the four corners of the amphitheater.

"The patch is characterized by exceptionally high concentrations of plastic, PCBs, chemical sludge, and other debris that has essentially been trapped by the currents of the North Pacific Gyre. It takes six years for the current to transport this garbage clockwise from the Aleutians, down the coast of North America to the equator, then west to Japan, and north to the Aleutians." Willow traced the circular track of the North Pacific Gyre with her laser pointer.

"Discarded fishing nets and buoys, plastic containers including billions of water and soft drink bottles, industrial and household plastics of all types, account for eighty percent of the pollution. As you might expect, the source of the garbage is vigorously debated. It is clear the problem is multi-dimensional - from inadequate waste management to illegal dumping by industrial and municipal polluters, ports, harbors, marinas, chemical and petroleum companies, fishing vessels, offshore oil and gas platforms, cargo ships, and perhaps billions of irresponsible people. The combined effect is devastating our oceans."

Willow took a break while a series of slides showing garbage floating on the ocean surface and the shores of Hawaii, Singapore,

Japan, Vietnam, Philippines, and Taiwan were displayed on the monitor.

"Now here is where it gets scary. Twenty years ago, in 2016, a multi-university study concluded *a hundred billion tons* of plastic had been produced since 1990. Eighty percent is no longer in use. Where did it go?" Willow paused long enough for the class to contemplate a response. She then answered her own question. "A small fraction of it went into a landfill. Most of it went into the ocean." Willow took a hard look at the faces of her students, assessing their reaction.

"Where are most of the industrial and population centers fronting the North Pacific?" she asked rhetorically. Seeing no hands, she answered the question. "The west coast of North America, Japan, Philippines, China, and Southeast Asia."

Willow stood and took a sip of water. Then she walked to the front of her desk and sat on the leading edge, stretching her legs while exploring her audience with a disquieted expression. Folding her arms across her chest, she continued.

"The Great Pacific Garbage Patch lies upon and below the surface of the water where both birds and marine life live, breed, and raise their young. Floating debris is clearly visible to boaters and low-flying aircraft, but cannot be detected by satellite. We've all seen graphic pictures of the garbage floating on the surface or littering our beaches. However, a greater portion of the patch is suspended in the water column, from just below the surface to the seabed thousands of feet below.

"How large is the Great Pacific Garbage Patch?" Willow sensed she had captured the undivided attention of her live audience.

"Thirty-six years ago, the North Pacific Gyre contained enough garbage to cover the entire state of Alaska - *five hundred thousand square mil*es."

The monitor displayed an outline of the state of Alaska hovering over the North Pacific Ocean. Several students muttered and moaned.

Another slide appeared on the monitor adjacent to the map. It was a graph spanning the years 2000 to 2050 on the horizontal scale and the size of the patch on the vertical scale.

"Fifteen years later, in 2015, the garbage patch had grown to one billion metric tons spread over an area *twice the size of Alaska* and encompassing the Hawaiian Islands."

Many of the students gasped at the specter when a second overlay of Alaska appeared on the map, enveloping the Hawaiian Islands.

"By 2025, the garbage patch had expanded to *four times* the size of Alaska with *two billion metric tons* of plastic waste circling the North Pacific."

Loud gasps and squeals of disgust erupted from the audience as two more overlays of Alaska appeared on the map.

"And this is what we're facing today." Willow's index finger dwelled over the year 2036. "The Great Pacific Garbage Patch is now *eight times the size of Alaska, four million square miles containing four billion tons of toxic plastics.*"

A total of *eight* overlays, each the size of the state of Alaska, covered virtually the entire North Pacific Ocean.

The audience was conspicuously silent - a sea of ghostly faces was transfixed on the monitors.

"Let's take a quick break," Sammy shouted. "Nice work, Professor. You really scared the crap out of everyone - more terrifying than a paranormal flick."

"It's not science fiction or paranormal psychosis, Sammy. This is really happening. Haven't you been to the beach lately? Every morning before the tourists arrive, they use a squadron of diesel tractors to clean up the crap that washed ashore with the high tide."

****

With the audience resettled, Willow continued her podcast.

"The impact of plastic pollution on our marine life, fish, cetaceans, birds, and mammals has been cataclysmic. Thousands of marine species have been declared extinct and thousands more are vanishing at an alarming rate. Salmon, tuna, billfish, jacks, cod, sardines, herring, crabs, and other food resources have spiraled into the extinction vortex. Dolphins, whales, seals, and walrus species are far past recovery. The last surviving polar bear perished in Winnipeg, Canada, ten years ago."

Willow pursed her lips, grimaced, and shook her head.

"What caused all this destruction?" Seeing no takers, she blurted, "Come on, people," with a display of frustration. "It's just plastic." There was no response.

"Photodegradation! How many of you have heard about photodegradation?"

A few students raised their hand.

"Life in the North Pacific Ocean is rapidly being exterminated due to the photodegradation of plastics. Photodegradation is the decomposition of plastic materials by ultraviolet light from the sun. Photodegraded plastics disintegrate into smaller and smaller confetti-like pieces while releasing their toxic chemicals into the ocean. This process continues down to the molecular level where the toxic soup is consumed by birds and marine organisms. It soon becomes part of the food chain."

Willow stopped for a moment to catch her breath. Looking out at her students, she believed she had captured their emotions.

"The Plastisphere is a name created by marine biologists for an ecological community of thousands of different organisms living and breeding entirely on photodegraded plastics. Many of these organisms are believed to pose a great risk to humans. Some are known to cause cancer and other life-threatening diseases in animals and humans. Other organisms thriving in the Plastisphere contain chemicals that can alter the DNA and genetic structure of certain organisms. This mutation process is known as horizontal gene transfer and, as in most bacteria, can often occur very quickly. There is evidence of horizontal gene transfer in thermal worms, and a few known extremophiles.

"Let's explore this phenomenon in greater detail with a discussion about sea skaters or halobates. Of the forty species of sea skaters, five live on the surface of the open ocean. These are the only known truly oceanic insects *and they are carnivores.*

"These small insects have a body length of about a quarter of an inch. They have long antennae and short front legs used for catching prey. They are very fast and can reach speeds of over three feet per second."

Willow took a moment for her students to process the math. "Can anyone tell me how fast that is, in miles per hour?"

There was a rush of digital button pushing and mumblings until someone shouted, "Two miles per hour!"

"That's right. About as fast you might stroll down the beach. They don't pose a danger to humans… *as long as their population remains relatively constant.*

"However, the females lay their eggs on floating plastic. The more plastic - the more eggs - the more eggs - the more sea skaters. Considering the rapidly increasing amount of plastic in the Great Pacific Garbage Patch, we may soon see a halobate explosion of biblical proportions - trillions upon trillions of carnivorous insects unlike the planet has ever experienced. It would be far larger and more devastating than the largest swarm of locusts. Anyone on or near the ocean would need to wear a mosquito net; otherwise, these little monsters would instantly invade their eyes, nostrils, and lungs. The victims would experience a terrifying death, first by going blind and then by suffocation."

"Cut!" Sammy shouted. "We need a short break. You certainly know how to hold an audience. Not a single person was nodding off. We need a short summary of what humans can expect if the problem is not resolved, how much time we have and what is or is not being done to address the problem."

"That's why I'm here."

"Okay. Let's wrap it up."

Willow collected her thoughts for the summary.

"Quiet on the set," Sammy shouted.

Willow looked into the camera with a steely, resolute expression.

"The scientific community is convinced there is a global catastrophe in the making. The scientific community has provided our world leaders indisputable proof and urged them to take immediate action before it is too late. So what exactly are they doing to address the problem?"

Willow took a moment of silence to let her audience consider the enormity of the issue.

"I'm afraid the answer is… *not much of anything.*"

There was a sudden outburst of rumblings, protestations, and discontent. Willow gave her audience a few moments to share their dismay and frustration.

"Let me be perfectly clear. There have been hundreds of surveys, scientific studies, computer models, and expert opinions by marine biologists and other scientists from NOAA, the United Nations, Scripps, Woods Hole, and many other prestigious institutions world-wide. They know the extent and urgency of the situation. Dozens of international conferences, treaties, agreements, and pledges have been drafted and signed. But when it comes to implementation of these agreements, everyone has their own agenda and justification for an exemption. Some of you may recall the UN Law of the Sea, and the International Whaling Commission ban on whaling. These treaties were ceremoniously signed by all the parties. NOAA, the UN, and the IWC immediately took to the stage and media, trumpeting around the world that the greatest threats facing mankind had been resolved. But the ink on these unenforceable decrees hadn't dried before most of the signatories had broken their promise.

"As for the Great Pacific Garbage Patch, and similar garbage patches in all our oceans and seas, our world leaders know the facts and the looming consequences. While the private sector has presented a few clean-up proposals, these ideas have never matured past the prototype phase and shortly thereafter died in some entrepreneurial dreamer's filing cabinet."

Willow glared into the camera, beseeching tears welling up in her eyes.

"I'm saddened to say this, but the human species is fractured. We profess brotherly love, but when push comes to shove, we turn our backs on our brothers. It's all about avarice, gluttony, selfishness, and reckless disregard for Mother Nature. It is no wonder that we humans, Homo sapiens, hold the dubious record for driving plant and animal species to their extinction."

Willow bowed her head and wiped away her tears.

Much of the audience did likewise.

CHAPTER 6
HORIZONTAL GENE TRANSFER

After securing the towing bridle, *Kanaloa* towed the habitat *Welina* to the Makai pier for decompression. The dockside tenders attached the gas supply hoses, habitat exhaust, electrical, and hard-wire communications lines.

"What's our decompression profile?" Davy shouted over the ship to shore intercom.

"You'll be decompressed using the standard saturation table for six hundred feet. Ten minutes per foot," Blake replied. "I'm taking the first watch."

"Gimme that figure in hours?" Davy asked impatiently.

"Come on, man. You should know this by heart. Four feet per hour. One hundred and fifty hours, assuming no one gets a hit. Just lay back and enjoy the ride. Maybe read a book or play a few games of chess. I know it's boring, but there's no alternative. You've done this many times, so just deal with it."

****

Even though he was exhausted, Bill couldn't get to sleep. The background noise was an orchestration of intermittent chit-chat, episodic hissing from the declining internal pressure coupled with the constant whirring of the carbon dioxide scrubbers. But what kept him from dozing off was the mystery of the creatures that consumed Karen. Unable to put it out of his mind, he shook the cobwebs from his head and walked toward the habitat laboratory.

He took a seat at his microscope and began to examine the objects Doctor Joe had given him. Suspended in the liquid preservative were several half-inch-long, translucent, worm-like creatures, a hagfish head, and a few pieces of hagfish flesh. Bill thought, with a little luck he could stay awake long enough to complete genomic DNA sequencing on these samples and maybe determine what role each one played in the death of Karen.

Using a pair of tweezers, he retrieved one of the seemingly dead wormlike creatures, rinsed it in saline solution and placed it on a digital scale. Recording his observations, Bill audibly described the first specimen.

"It looks like a tardigrade but it is significantly larger. It weighs six hundred and five milligrams." He proceeded to take measurements.

"The body is translucent, twelve millimeters long and two millimeters wide. I've never seen or read about this creature. Maybe it's a new species." The thought of such a rare discovery momentarily took his breath.

Bill continued with his recording. "These organisms are extremophiles, one of just a few organisms that have survived all major extinction events. They're born with about forty-thousand cells, live for up to two years, and die with the same number of cells they had when they were born."

As Bill went about recording his observations, beads of anticipation rolled off his forehead. He gingerly placed the creature under his microscope and focused the optics on the specimen.

"Jesus, this thing is still alive! He's moving his head and body like a freshly caught fish."

Bill maneuvered the dark-colored head to better inspect the mouthparts. At first, the image was out of focus, but as he brought the creature's mouth into view, nothing could have shocked him more.

"Bloody hell! This bastard has an impressive set of choppers. There's an upper and lower row of triangular-shaped teeth with serrated edges - ideal for a carnivore. I've never heard of anything like this in my entire life. Tardigrades don't have teeth. This is incredible. It must be a new species. Let's see if he likes to eat hagfish?"

Bill cut off a small piece of hagfish flesh and placed it next to the creature.

"My God! He's all over the hagfish like a ravenous lion."

As he continued to observe the rapacious creature under magnification, he became mesmerized by its distinctly unique characteristics. In all his years, he had never seen anything like this grotesque organism.

"Okay, dinner is over. It's time to determine your make and model."

Bill placed the squiggling sample in a desiccating chamber and dialed in the timer. Minutes later, he removed a small round ball. The creature had entered a state of cryptobiosis. Bill then crushed the body to a fine powder, placed the substance in a test tube, and added the DNA amplifier.

****

"Hey, Bill. What are you up to?" Bill was startled at the sudden appearance of Walt climbing through the laboratory hatchway.

"I've been analyzing the samples Doctor Joe provided. One of the specimens has me confused. It looks like a tardigrade, but he's ten times larger and has a well-developed set of teeth. There is no doubt he's a carnivore. He gobbled up a bit of hagfish flesh in a few seconds."

"Do you think it's a new species or a mutation?"

"We'll know soon. I'm prepping the specimen for a DNA test. You saw what happened to Karen. What do you make of this?" Bill replayed the video of the specimen's teeth. "Tell me I'm hallucinating."

"Mother Mary!" Walt lurched back, profoundly befuddled.

"Big teeth, eh?" Bill sneered.

"Oh, yeah." Walt shook his head in disbelief. "His teeth are serrated, like a tiger shark. It might be a mutation."

"At first, I thought it was a new species. This monster looks like a gargantuan tardigrade with a massive set of dentures. But truthfully, Walt, I don't know what this is. We'll have to wait for the DNA results."

"What can I do to help? I'm pretty handy in the lab and I've done a fair amount of DNA tests."

"You can start by taking a good look at this hagfish head, and then prepare it for DNA analysis. I'm ready to put this organism in the sequencer."

Walt took a seat at the microscope and maneuvered the hagfish head under the magnification optics. He began his examination of the mouth. Taking a pair of tweezers, he opened the mouthparts to view the teeth.

Mumbling to himself, Walter recited his observations. "There is nothing new here - two rows of comb-shaped tooth-like structures embedded in cartilaginous plates that open and close like a fist. I'm perplexed as to why the hagfish attacked Karen. Maybe it was the smell of blood in the water."

His scrutiny was then drawn to the eye-spots. "This doesn't look right."

Using a pointed scalpel, he carefully made a circular incision around one of the dark spheres looking for indications of extra-ocular muscles.

"Holy shit!" Filled with incertitude, Walt shook his head in disbelief. "These eyes have a lens."

Searching deeper into the tissues he found the next anomaly. "Extraocular muscles! This species has peripheral vision. He can probably move his eyes and focus on an object, even a moving target."

Bill interrupted Walter's train of thought. "Hey, you look like you just saw a naked lady. What's up with the hagfish?"

"The eyes. They're complex. This one has a lens and the muscle to focus."

"Hagfish eyes are virtually useless. They don't have lenses and they can't resolve images!" Bill countered.

"Be my guest." Walt pointed to the microscope and handed Bill the scalpel.

Still skeptical, Bill looked at the specimen. "Well, I'll be crackers." Bill gave Walt a gratuitous grin. "Well done, mate. Brilliant."

"Thanks, Bill. I'll get a sample prepped for DNA. Let me know when I can use the sequencer."

****

The sequencer sounded off with a pair of chimes indicating the genomic DNA test was finished.

"I've got the printout," Bill shouted while letting the stream of paper flow smoothly through his fingertips.

Scanning the results, Bill's eyes suddenly widened.

"This confirms it. Our critter is a tardigrade. There's a footnote that indicates this is a genetically mutated specimen. Oh, no. This is not good." Bill's face soured. "There's another footnote. It says trace amounts of PCBs and polystyrene derivatives were identified." Tears welled up in Bill's eyes and he shook his head.

Walt put his arm on Bill's shoulder.

"This is definitely a mutation, probably due to the toxic effects of photodegraded plastics. You know what this means?"

Stumped, Walter shrugged his shoulders.

"This is potentially an ecological thunderstorm." Bill waved the computer printout above his head. "This information may have global implications. It suggests that pollution of the marine environment is causing some organisms to adapt to the toxic effects much faster and more dramatically than ever thought possible. This is dangerous data, Walt. We've got to keep it to ourselves. We cannot speak about this to anyone. It must remain a secret. Our lives and those of our loved ones could be at risk. Do you understand?"

"Sure, Bill. Whatever you say."

"Good. Now let's test the hagfish. Maybe we'll get some better news."

****

The atmosphere was suddenly drained of energy. While Walt initiated the hagfish DNA sequence, Bill retrieved the thumb drive from the video recorder, slid it into his pocket and inserted a fresh drive. Several silent minutes passed before the ring of the computer signaled the DNA sequence for the hagfish was complete.

"Hagfish DNA on the way," Walt attested.

Hagfish are eel-shaped, slime-producing marine fish. They are the only living animals that have a skull but no vertebral column. The largest known species can reach over four feet in length. The common Pacific species, *E. stoutii,* typically range from one to two feet in length. As scavengers, they quickly respond to the scent of blood and can survive many months between feedings. However, when they do eat, their feeding behavior is extremely vigorous.

"Bill, here comes the output."

"I got it," Bill said. Holding one end in his right hand, he ran his left hand down the printout. Halfway down the list was an asterisk.

Next to it was the genomic name of the sample. "I am surprised, but the genomic DNA doesn't lie. It says this creature is a Pacific hagfish. They're the dominant scavenger in the Pacific."

"But hagfish don't attack living organisms or people. At least that's what the books say." Walt was puzzled.

"There is some evidence to the contrary. They've been known to attack several bottom dwellers such as red bandfish, and like a pack of hungry wolves, they form up into large schools to attack wounded marine animals including cetaceans and seals."

"What about the eyes? That's totally contradictory to hagfish anatomy. What else does the report indicate?" Walt asked.

Wrinkling his brow, Bill shrugged his shoulders and scanned down the computer print-out.

"There's a footnote that says there is evidence of horizontal gene transfer - eight percent. It also found traces of PCBs and polystyrene. That's all there is. We'll have to speculate as to why they have complex eyes," Bill observed.

"I don't know what to make of all this. First, the DNA points to the hagfish as the creature that initially attacked Karen. Now we learn that tardigrades were likely the monsters that finished the…" Walter froze, unable to complete his thought. His imagination entered a dispirited cloud.

"Are you okay?" Bill asked.

Walter regained his composure and changed the subject, trying his best to avoid dealing with the magnitude of the moment.

"I'm from the old school. I don't understand all of Mother Nature's mysteries. Some of this DNA research is mind-boggling. Christ, for fifty dollars, they can break down your ancestry to within a half-percentage point. I was blown away when I learned I was nine percent African. My great-great-great granddaddy musta been messing around with some of those beautifully black Georgia peaches and then oops, he knocks one up. What a rascal. What's your DNA profile? I bet you've got some super genes like Einstein or Stephen Hawking."

"Nope. Mostly British with a little Italian and American Indian. My ancestors came over on the Mayflower in 1630 and settled in Massachusetts."

"They must have dealt with some horrendous hardships."

"Like most pilgrims and explorers of that time, they either starved, froze, or died from a lethal disease or an arrow from an outraged native. But a few of the more resilient pilgrims overcame the environmental hardships. They adapted and survived. They learned how to overcome the hardships and eventually thrived - built an entire nation of five hundred million people."

"I imagine those human qualities qualify us as extremophiles."

Spellbound, Bill and Walt were momentarily speechless, lost in their breaking discoveries. Indeed, their findings represented a momentous milestone in the annals of evolutionary science, although it was not likely to inspire accolades or admiration.

What they had discovered, while decompressing their bodies from a deep saturation dive, was a paradigm shift in the trajectory of life on the planet. Sadly, that phylogenic change was not only irreparable - it was perpetrated by Homo sapiens - the brightest, most innovative, and sadly, the most rapacious species on the planet.

CHAPTER 7

MURDER ON THE LIKE-LIKE HIGHWAY

"What time is it?" Willow yawned and stretched out her arms like a soaring eagle.

"Almost eight o'clock. It's Saturday, and we slept in. I have a surprise for us," Blake snuggled and whispered in Willow's ear.

"Darling, I love your surprises."

"You know, next month is our third anniversary of being together, so I thought about making reservations at the new Royal Chateau on the Chuuk Islands. That's where we first met, remember, when you and one of your grad students, Christy something or other, joined me on a wreck dive to a Japanese battleship. We've never been back, so I thought you might enjoy some sightseeing and maybe see if Captain Henry is still hosting lagoon dive trips aboard *Goldilocks*. The hotel has only been open a few months. I hear they have the most magnificent ocean view suites in the world and thick, down-filled comforters - the squishy kind you can sink into up to your ears."

"Nothing is more enticing than being in a squishy bed with my man." Willow wiggled her fanny into Blake's loins while he wrapped his arms around her waist. "I love it when your warm breath flows across the back of my neck. It's a magical turn-on. Humm."

"We can spend a week relaxing by the pool or scuba diving or whatever. They've got seven swimming pools and a wonderful snorkeling reef. We can rent a boat if you want to do some exploring - maybe find a secluded beach - someplace where we can be alone and celebrate three wonderful years together."

"That would be fabulous. We need some private time - no midnight phone calls. When do we leave?"

"Let's figure out the best date."

"Shucks, honey, that gives us plenty of time to practice. Come to me, lover boy." Willow rolled over facing Blake and began her ritual *me love you longtime* massage.

"Wanna fiddle around before breakfast?"

"Fiddle - faddle - jump in the saddle," Blake chuckled.

"Silly poet. We have so much fun in bed. It's the most wonderful place in my world. Do you like that?" Their passion deepened.

"Oh, yeah. Can't you see you're driving me crazy." Blake moved closer and they exchanged a long, luscious kiss.

Willow yanked off the covers, rested her head on Blake's chest and methodically twirled her index finger down his abdomen.

"I could stay here forever. I'm so happy. You make my life complete. I love you so much." Abruptly, she sat upright, pulled off her nightgown and gave Blake a sexy pose. "This is such a beautiful place to love the man of my dreams. I want to stay here forever."

"Forever is a long time. I've loved you too long to worry about tomorrow. Who knows what's ahead. Let's enjoy what we have - live in the moment. It's ours now - let's not worry about the future. Besides, neither of us has a crystal ball. We can chart a course but the winds and tides may not take us there."

"I know. You're a realist. But I can dream and you can too. So give me a kiss and I'll take you to wonderland." She cupped her palms over his cheeks and pulled him to her breasts. "How about a little revelry before breakfast?"

Blake was spellbound by her seductive charms.

"Just lay back and enjoy." She swirled the tip of her tongue across her lips until they shone in the morning sunlight. Then, with a yearning smile, she gazed down and purred, "Pour moi?" She coyly raised her eyebrows and puckered her wet lips.

"Oui, pour mon amour."

"Hmm. Yummy! I'm going to take you to a magical place," she cooed.

"What about you?"

"I'm just going to warm you up."

"I'm already warmed up."

"Then come to me, my prince. Come to me."

****

"Race you to the shower!" Willow yelled, jumping out of bed.

"Hey, that's cheating. You got a head start."

"Come on. Wash my back, and I'll do yours."

Blake was halfway to the shower when the phone rang.

"I'll get it," Blake mumbled. "It better not be one of those solar panel telemarketers. It's Saturday for Pete's sake. Hello." Blake answered briskly.

"Blake, it's MaryJo, MaryJo Butler."

"Well helllooo, MaryJo. How's our favorite benefactor? Are you in Honolulu?"

"Charlie and I had some business with a delegation from the IWC. It's always contentious dealing with these mucky-mucks from the International Whaling Commission. The meeting was awkward and probably a waste of our time, but we have to keep up the pressure."

"Willow is in the shower. Hold on a second while I put you on the speaker. Willow," Blake yelled. "It's MaryJo Butler. Come listen to what she has to say."

Turning his attention back to MaryJo, Blake continued. "Willow is listening in. I know she'd love to speak with you."

"Hi, MaryJo." Willow said, wrapping a large towel around her torso. "It's great to hear from you. How's Charlie? We miss his sense of humor."

"He's fine. That man is like a rock. He wakes up no different from when he went to bed." MaryJo chuckled.

At five-foot two and a hundred and fifteen pounds, MaryJo Butler might have been small in stature, but she was a heavyweight with a mighty big voice in the global movement to save the dolphins. As a graduate of Amherst, she was a highly principled woman. And even though she was losing the battle to save the smartest animal in the oceans, she pressed forward with determination and resolve.

On the other hand, her husband Charlie was a giant of a man with the heart of an angel. While earning his MBA from Yale, he and MaryJo met at a Woods Hole symposium and were married three months later. Their first child was stillborn and MaryJo was unable to conceive more children. That didn't stop Charlie or MaryJo. Charlie joined a prestigious Wall Street firm and the newlyweds immediately began adopting children - eight of them. After twenty years, Charlie left the financial world with a billion-dollar net worth and together, he and MaryJo formed the Rescue Me Foundation. Their mission was well defined by their watchword. *"Every dolphin saved brings a smile to the planet."* Charlie and MaryJo were also significant benefactors for the Makai Institute of Marine Technology.

"Charlie and I are traveling aboard *Rescue Me*. We arrived yesterday after an eight-day voyage from Taiji. It's wonderful to be back in friendly waters."

"Blake and I are quite familiar with the Taiji problem. It's a disgrace to the human race. How did it go?"

"The Taiji dolphin killers hate our guts. They're heathens, obsessed with the slaughter of dolphins. We tried everything possible to disrupt their monthly hunt, but the government dispatched a couple of armed police patrol boats and drove us off under the threat of gunfire and imprisonment. One of the patrol boats tried to ram us."

As her anger grew, her voice broke to a higher octave. "We took some gruesome video of the killing cove. Hundreds of dolphins, adults, mothers, and babies, hysterically thrashing about as one by one they were harpooned or whacked with a machete. It's like that every month. It's worse than anything you could imagine." MaryJo's voice trailed off and she began to sob.

"That is very depressing." Willow dabbed the tears pooling in her eyes. "I read about your efforts. You and Charlie should be proud of what you've accomplished. I'm saddened to learn about the loss of our cetacean friends. What a horrible dilemma. What are you and Charlie going to do? Is there anything Blake and I can do to help?"

"We've tried just about everything to stop the senseless killing, but the Japanese government insists the fishermen have a cultural right to continue slaughtering these helpless animals. That's pure bullshit. They only started hunting dolphins in the 1970s. We've been somewhat successful in stopping the sale of dolphins for tourist attractions. But after sixty years of indiscriminate hunting, oceanic pollution, deadly sonic booms, and collateral damage from commercial fishing operations, the dolphin populations are decimated. Our last official count was two years ago. The Pacific bottlenose population is virtually extinct - fewer than a thousand individuals. That's not enough to sustain the species."

"That's dreadful. I know how much effort and resources you and Charlie have put into this mission. It saddens Blake and me to learn the extent to which greed drives some men. I reckon we're not the smartest species on the planet."

Sniffling, MaryJo continued. "We're tired but not giving up. Charlie and I are together on this mission. We've made many more enemies than friends. The Japanese of Taiji hate our guts and so do most of the members of the IWC. They tolerate us at environmental meetings and IWC and UN conferences, but their smiles and words are insincere, just for the media. Last year Charlie and I were threatened several times. Two of our team members have been murdered. Jane Pitson, Director of our program in St. Lucia, was killed two years ago - fatally shot while driving home. The police said it was a random killing - never did a damn thing. A year later Jenny Day, one of our roving ambassadors, was strangled on a Tel Aviv beach."

"Jenny Day! Murdered? That is so sad. Blake and I knew her. She used to work at the university, in the marine aquaculture department."

"She was a renowned dolphin advocate. No one has ever been charged. And some of our other associates have received death threats too. It's a war. And we're gonna continue the fight. *Rescue Me* needs some engine work, so we'll be here for a few more days. Maybe we could get together for a drink or dinner?"

"Sure, how about tomorrow evening? We'll meet you at Buzzy's Steak House in Lanikai. I think you've been there before."

"That sounds terrific."

"Good. It will be nice to see you guys again."

****

Blake tossed his car keys to the valet while Willow took his arm and sashayed up the tile stairs to the main entrance of Buzzy's Steak House.

The Matre'd escorted the couple to an ocean view table for four, handed out menus and took their drink orders. The Hawaiian moon was peeking upward from behind the horizon while the sweet scent of plumeria blossoms waltzed across the dining room.

"Willow, you look absolutely stunning in that dress, and those sexy stilettos. Wow. You are the most beautiful woman in the world."

"Flatterer." Willow teased. "You better save room for my dessert."

"I never let dinner spoil dessert," Blake snickered.

For the next hour, they continued to embrace the ambiance of the evening while listening to soft Hawaiian music.

"What time did MaryJo say they'd meet us for dinner?" Blake looked at his watch and took another sip of his second mai-tai.

"Seven thirty. They're over an hour late. I'll give them a call?"

Willow dialed MaryJo's number and gave Blake a smile upon hearing the first ringtone. On the fourth ringtone, the voice mail kicked in and Willow left a short message.

"They must be running late. It's almost nine. Why don't we eat? They probably got distracted by some emergency. What suits your taste buds?" Blake asked.

"*Opakapaka.* Pink snapper is my favorite. How about you?"

"Langostino à la Kailua. The last time I had them was in Kona, years ago. Tiny little critters, but oh, so delicious with mango salsa and mild chili's."

"And dessert. What's your pleasure?" Willow winked.

"I thought we already agreed on dessert." Blake and Willow giggled together.

"You know, I'm still quite puzzled about the death of Karen Savoy. We know she was attacked by some type of marine animal or animals. Do you have any idea what sort of creature could do that to a diver - a diver wearing a dry suit?" Blake asked.

Willow had second thoughts about telling Blake what she and Carla had discovered about the pupu diver, but because of the possible repercussions, even dangers, they had both promised not to speak of it until someone came forward with data that would support their findings.

"I have some ideas, nothing proven, mind you. I'm still working on them. I'll let you know if it pans out."

"You know Doctor Joe retrieved some hagfish specimens, and a few other worm-like creatures. He found them inside Karen's dry suit. I think he gave them to Bill Knight."

A rush of anxiety dashed across Willow's shoulders. She took a long swallow of her drink and forced herself to remain composed. "What did Bill do with the samples?" Willow asked in a quaking voice.

"I'm not sure. I assume he took them to his lab in Santa Barbara."

"Yeah, I'm curious about what he may have found. I'm sure he would have contacted me if it was important. Here comes our dinner. I'm starving."

****

The happy couple ate their dinners while enjoying the warm ocean breeze and Hawaiian love songs.

"Are you about ready to head home?" Blake asked. "It's after ten."

"I'm worried about MaryJo and Charlie. It's not like them to forget. And if they had something more important, they would have called."

"Let's head home. You can call them again from the car."

****

The sun was just breaking the horizon when the phone rang. Blake stirred and looked at his watch. "Christ, it's five-thirty in the morning. Who could be calling at this hour? Hello. Who's this calling so early?"

"This is Lieutenant Singer, Honolulu police department. Is Willow Parker there?"

"What is this about?"

"I need to speak with Willow Parker about an accident."

Willow began to stir when she heard Blake take the call.

"She's right here. Hold on. Willow, wake up. It's the police: something about an accident."

"What? Who's calling?"

Willow took the phone. "Hello. This is Willow Parker. What is this about?"

"There has been an accident on the Likelike Highway. Charles and MaryJo Butler."

"Oh, no. That's impossible." Willow began to shake.

"I'm afraid so. Their rental car missed one of the hairpin curves around seven last night. They plunged down a cliff near the summit. There was an explosion. They both died instantly."

"We were waiting for them at Buzzy's, for dinner. They never showed up. What an injustice. They were the most generous, and compassionate people imaginable. That is terrible news. How did you get my phone number?"

"We have video from the Ala Moana harbor showing them leaving their vessel with three unidentified men wearing black slacks and dark blue hoodies. We couldn't see their faces or any other identifying marks. They got into a black SUV and left. We found MaryJo's purse on their vessel and retrieved her cell phone. We replayed your voice message and got your cell number. It did not appear to be a robbery. It was more likely a kidnapping. We have no idea how they wound up in a rental car at the bottom of the cliff."

****

Willow couldn't sleep. The suspicious deaths of her good friends Charlie and MaryJo Butler bored a stinging hole in her heart. And what Blake had said about the samples that Doctor Joe gave to Bill Knight exacerbated the torment.

She got out of bed and walked to the kitchen. Filling a tall glass with cold tap water, she looked at the wall clock. It was four in the morning. After a quick moment of mental arithmetic, she realized it was seven in the morning in Santa Barbara. She grabbed her cell phone from the nearby counter and seated herself at the kitchen table. It took a few moments to look up and dial Bill Knight's phone number.

Bill answered his phone on the fourth ring.

"Hello, Bill. It's Willow."

"Hello, Willow. You're up early."

"I can't sleep. I was thinking about Karen and trying to come to grips with the cause of her death. Blake told me Doctor Joe gave you some samples of organisms he found inside her dry suit. I was curious to know if you could tell me anything about them."

There was a protracted period of silence before Bill mumbled. "Mutated hagfish and tardigrades. That's all I can tell you over the phone."

Stunned beyond her sensibilities, there was a long pause. Willow gasped and silently disengaged from the tempo of the conversation.

"Willow, are you okay?"

Willow forced herself to return to the conversation.

"Yes Bill. I'm okay. Just shocked and numb. I can't talk now. I'll get back to you soon."

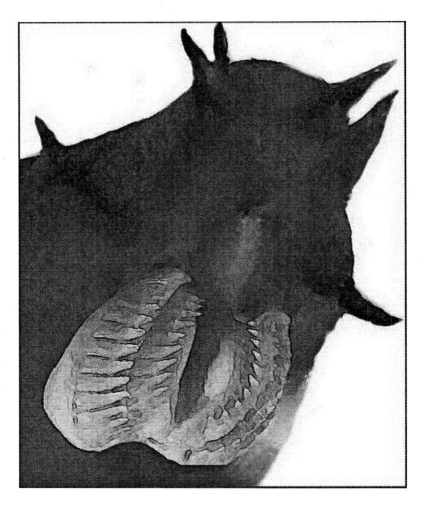

Hagfigh jaws

CHAPTER 8

BLOODWORMS GONE WILD

Wearing a dark blue suit, white shirt, red tie, and a jubilant grin, Byron Sylvester rushed from the elevator onto King Street where he hailed a taxi. After a red-eye from Los Angeles to Honolulu followed by five hours of interviews with the management staff, he was ready for a hot shower and a nap.

"Where to?" asked the Filipino driver while putting on his best happy-face.

"Hyatt Regency."

"Okey-dokey." The musky fragrance of cheap perfume rushed across Byron's olfactory senses. The driver funneled the Prius into mid-afternoon traffic and merged onto Kalakakua Avenue toward Waikiki beach.

"Where you from?" asked the driver.

"California."

"North or South?"

"Middle. San Luis Obispo."

"Is your first time Honolulu?" The driver spoke in fractured phrases.

"I came here on vacation once, with my parents a long time ago. I've been busy with college since then."

"Business or playtime?"

"Today's business is over. I'm pooped and need a nap." Byron removed his fire-engine-red power tie and put it in his suit jacket pocket.

"We here, now," the driver said, pulling into the circular driveway. Turning off his meter, he said, "Twenty dollar, please."

Unwilling to engage the driver about the obvious overcharge, Byron pulled a twenty from his wallet, paid, and entered the hotel.

****

It was four o'clock in a late June afternoon when Byron stepped inside his suite at the Hyatt. Kicking off his shoes, he flopped on the king-size bed and stared at the whitewashed ceiling. "God damn!" he called out. "It's great to be alive."

At six-feet and one hundred and seventy pounds, his athletic body was trim and firm. His handsome face, blue eyes, contagious grin, and easygoing disposition helped him earn the respect of his peers and flirtatious smiles from the ladies. Now, at the age of twenty-six, he had secured a high-paying opportunity to work in his field of expertise - legal marijuana - weed.

He was in his prime - more ambitious and confident than most. He was about to embark on a new phase of his life. This was his time - he could feel it in his bones - wealth, power and prestige were his destiny.

Yet, in the back of his mind was the nagging picture of his beginnings on the streets of Los Angeles - the street gangs, drug dealers, pimps, and fractured souls walking aimlessly down Hollywood Boulevard. At the age of seventeen, Byron found a way out of the misery by joining the Marine Corps. Through the force of his own will, he had scratched, kicked, and gouged his way to the top of the mountain. Using his VA benefits, a part-time job, and a hundred thousand dollars in student loans, he managed to complete his college education and begin his professional business career.

****

Byron awakened with the late afternoon sun streaming in through the sliding glass door. Stepping out onto the balcony, he was aroused by the immensity and power of the Pacific Ocean. It was a beautiful day in Honolulu - a giant leap from the pernicious streets of LA.

As he scanned the beach, a gentle breeze rappelled cross his face. Swooping bands of orange and red clouds stretched across the western sky. Dozens of sailboats, large and small, dotted the seascape - their mainsails and genoas billowing on the tack. On the beach, a ragtag gathering of rambunctious young men stumbled across the Waikiki sand chasing a tumbling football. Clusters of young women lay face down on their towels, tanning their glistening, oil-coated bodies in the late afternoon sun.

Byron felt a stirring in his loins. Stepping into the white-tiled shower, he let the clear hot water splash against his back for several minutes while washing his face, chest, and legs. Memories of rust-colored water dripping from a broken faucet in his LA bathroom flashed before him. When finished with his shower, he stood in front of the mirror and shaved. Wiping away the remains of his shaving cream, he cast off the images of his past, and then splashed a generous portion of his favorite cologne on his face.

Pausing to admire himself in the mirror, Byron pushed out his chest, sucked in his stomach, and proclaimed, "Hot damn! You're one good-looking, sweet-smelling dude. It sure is great to be living in the land of the free and home of the brave."

After dressing in knee-length khaki shorts, a blue, short-sleeved linen shirt, and blue canvas deck shoes, he checked his watch. It was time to work his magic.

Byron felt a rush of inspiration as he rode the elevator to the ground floor. He could almost taste success - this was his time - he was cocksure of it.

He strolled into the poolside lounge appropriately named Bikini's and took a seat at the teakwood bar. Running his eyes over the scantily-clad women in the courtyard, he indulged the thought that tonight he was going to get lucky.

"What'll it be, mister?"

"As they say, when in Rome do what the Romans do. I'll have a strong mai-tai."

"Double mai-tai. Yes, sir." Byron took note of the barkeep's name tag, Ringo.

"What brings you to Honolulu?" Ringo asked as he placed the icy mai-tai and a small cup of macadamia nuts on the bar.

"Business, but I hear this is a good place to meet the ladies."

"Depends on your appetite. Most are on vacation. Some are married, but more are single. We don't run a dating service, but you might find what you're looking for right here."

"I understand," Byron said, sipping his drink. As he looked out at the sunbathers, a shot of adrenaline sailed through his bones and he suddenly felt invincible, like an alpha-male wolf tracking the irresistible scent of a flirtatious female.

An hour and another mai-tai later, Byron eyed a tall brunette taking a seat a few stools to his left. She hiked her bright red skirt exposing a delicious thigh, crossed her long legs and leaned one elbow on the bar. "Ringo, I'd like a glass of Chardonnay, please."

"Coming right up, Miss Templeton."

When her drink arrived, she looked at Byron over her right shoulder and smiled. He held her gaze. She looked stunning in her low-cut dress, strappy high-heels and a gold necklace with a heavy pendant bobbing across her delectable cleavage. This might be the one, he thought as he stood and picked up his drink.

"May I join you?"

"Please do. I'm Diane, what's your name?"

"Byron."

"What shall we drink to tonight, Byron?"

"Let's see. How about we celebrate a new beginning - a fresh start to the rest of our lives?"

"To a new start," said Diane, raising her glass. "So, what brings you to Honolulu?"

"My first real job."

"What kind of job?"

"I'm in the weed business."

Diane raised her impish eyebrows.

"I've accepted a new position for NoKaOi Pharma. They're one of the two medical marijuana licensees in Oahu. They have a twenty-thousand-square-foot indoor hydroponic cultivation plant, and I'm responsible for making the best use of every square foot."

"I don't trip very often. But when I do, I want the best. When it comes to soothing the body, mind, and spirit, why use anything less? Do you have any samples?" Diane smiled and fluttered her lashes in a seductive, neoclassical manner.

"As a matter of fact, I do. My new boss gave me a few THC vaping oils and one of their new pipes. Like you, I only want the best. I never smoke the buds. Vaping is much easier on the lungs - it doesn't bite. And after three or four puffs, you're good to go."

"Maybe you and I could party. I know a great little beach, very private."

Intuitively, Byron now believed he was on his way to fulfilling his lascivious wish.

"Why don't we have dinner first? I haven't eaten all day. After a six-hour flight and five hours of interviews, I'm starved."

"That would be nice. I've eaten here often - the service is excellent. Let's get a table?"

The handsome couple left the bar and walked up to the restaurant entrance.

"Something quiet with an ocean view?" Byron slipped a ten-dollar bill into the hand of the Maitre d' and they were promptly escorted to a table facing the magnificent sunset.

"How's this, sir?"

"Excellent and the sunset is a perfect touch," Byron smiled.

Diane settled into her chair.

"Do you live in Honolulu or are you on vacation?" Byron asked.

"I was born and raised here. My dad was a career naval officer, a dentist. We were based near Pearl Harbor. I guess you could say I'm a Navy brat. But I try hard not to let the brat out, especially at night," Diane giggled.

"You look off the charts in that dress. What do you wear during the day?"

"I'm a certified hair stylist. I work in the financial district. Professional women demand the best and the compensation is much better than salons in the suburbs."

The waiter appeared, took their dinner orders, and withdrew.

"When are you moving to Honolulu?" Diane inquired.

"First, I have to find an apartment. Maybe you could point me in the right direction?"

"I live in a nice complex, close to good restaurants and bars. You should check it out."

As the evening progressed, they drew closer. Their discourse became spontaneous, as though they had known each other for years. As the time passed, they quickly discovered they had much in common; their likes, dislikes, political and lifestyle choices synced perfectly.

"Would you like a nightcap?" Byron asked, slightly intoxicated by the liquor and Diane's obvious coquetry. The thought of making love with her was infatuating.

"I'd rather escort you to my favorite beach and try some of your NoKaOi molasses. My car is in the parking lot. We can grab a bottle of your favorite beverage on the way."

"I didn't bring my bathing suit."

"I didn't either. But no worries mate, as they say down under. There's seldom anyone on this beach after dark and I know of a secret spot where no one will disturb us. It's quiet, the perfect spot for tokers and lovers."

"Why not your apartment?"

"I've got a roommate and she's got a boyfriend spending the night. I promised her I'd give her some privacy. *ComeonIwannalaya*. We're wasting time."

"You speak Hawaiian quite well." Byron's libido soared as Diane took hold of his hand and escorted him to the parking lot.

Diane giggled. "That's not really Hawaiian. It's more of an invitation. Look at that moon. Don't you just love the moon on a clear night?" She turned to face Byron and kissed him on the mouth. "Yummy. You're a good kisser. I like that."

After purchasing a bottle of Don Julio tequila, they drove along the coast toward Diane's secluded beach. Byron looked out to sea, mesmerized by the effervescent waves breaking across the rocky shoreline, portending an enchanting conclusion to his first night in Honolulu.

"What's the name of this beach?" Byron asked as Diane turned off the coast highway onto a narrow descending roadway.

"Hanauma Bay. It used to be a favorite for locals and tourists, but the reef died and the colorful fish left. We'll have to hike a little to get down to the beach. That's why it's so private. I'll grab a blanket. You bring the hooch and NoKaOi."

"This place is fabulous. Look, at the bioluminescence as the waves surge up the sand. It's like magic," Byron exclaimed as he followed Diane down the trail to the beach.

"Just a little further, toward the cliff. There's a small cave. It's perfect for a secret rendezvous," Diane chuckled. "Here we are. Watch your head."

"You've been here before."

"A few times. It's much more romantic than a noisy bedroom. To me, it's like being in a movie. Help me spread the blanket. Then we can have a drink and test-drive some of your molasses."

Byron opened the tequila, took a long swig, and passed the bottle to Diane. She looked up to the stars. Reflections of moonbeams bounced off her eyes, making them sparkle like diamonds. She put the neck of the bottle into her mouth and swallowed several gulps.

"Ahhh! That's sooo smooth. Expensive, but worth every drop."

"Here, I've loaded a caplet of NoKaOi Gold. It's pretty strong so take it easy. Two or three puffs and you'll be anywhere your thoughts will take you."

Diane inhaled three long puffs from the vape pipe and leaned back, pulling Byron forward until their lips met in a passionate, waterlogged kiss. Seconds later, she began to tease, exploring his body with her hand and arching her body in rhythmic submission.

Their foreplay intensified until they frantically disrobed, locked legs and consummated their sexcapade in a flurry of Hanauma Bay sand.

****

Diane took a long drag on the vape pipe, and with an appreciative smile, placed her head on Byron's shoulder.

"You like?"

"Oui. Merci beaucoup, mademoiselle."

"God, I love it when you talk dirty."

"That's French," Byron snickered.

"Mademoiselle is going for a swim. Wanna join me?" Diane took another hit and chased it with a long swallow of tequila.

"I've never gone naked on the beach," Byron grumbled.

"Come on. Don't be shy. Look, see me. I'm letting it all hang out." Diane shook her delectable boobs and struck a flirtatious pose. "Race you to the water."

Diane rushed to the water's edge, letting the incoming wave roll up her ankles.

"The water is perfect. I'm going for a dip." She knelt, raised her arms above her head and rolled forward into the shallows. After a couple of strokes, she turned to look back at Byron. "Come to Mademoiselle. Mademoiselle needs a kiss."

"You should have been an actress. You've got the looks, the legs, and great tits." Byron fell head-first into the shore break and swam to Diane. When he reached her, they embraced.

As their tongues danced, they stumbled back toward the beach where Byron gently lowered Diane to the wet sand.

"I've never done it like this before," Diane whispered in his ear. "But don't stop loving me."

Their passion quickly transitioned into NaKaOi, and tequila-powered overdrive. The combination of her sexual craving with the release of dopamine, oxytocin, and endorphins into her brain, rendered her completely preoccupied, so much so, that she was oblivious to the subtle movements beneath her backside as three slimy creatures burrowed their way through the wet sand directly under her gyrating torso.

Like a perfectly choreographed recital, the bloodworms simultaneously snapped their long venomous fangs into her flesh - one on her left thigh, another to her buttocks, and the third to her shoulder.

Leaping to her feet, Diane bellowed a painful scream. "Aaaeee, Aaaeee," she shrieked while furiously spinning in sporadic circles and thrashing her arms to her backside.

For a moment, Byron failed to comprehend the situation. His first thought was that she was having some sort of seizure. But then, as she spun round and round, he saw the three bloodworms hooked into her body.

"Get them off! Aaaeee. Oh God. Get them off. Aaaeee!" Diane shouted hysterically.

Byron grasped one of the bloodworms, but it was too slimy to secure. He tried a second and third time, but it slipped through his grasp.

Diane slumped to her knees, writhing in excruciating pain. "Aaaeee, Eeeaaa. Help me." She suddenly vomited and convulsed from head toe, like a grand mal seizure. She then fell forward, planted the side of her face into the sand. Still shaking uncontrollably, she passed out.

Shocked at the carnage, Byron was momentarily dazed. Shaking his head, he tried to envision the best course of action. He raced to the blanket, retrieved his phone and dialed 911.

"911. What is your emergency?"

"I need an ambulance, immediately," he screamed. "My girlfriend has been attacked by some kind of pink-colored snakes; they've attached themselves to her body. She's unconscious on the beach. Hurry. I'm afraid she might die."

"Slow down. Where are you?"

"Hanauma Bay. On the beach. Please hurry."

"Stay with her. An ambulance will be there shortly."

Byron pulled on his shorts and shirt, grabbed the blanket and dashed back to Diane. She remained unconscious, face down while the bloodworms continued to suckle - the color of their slimy bodies turning from a soft pink to a bright red as they gorged themselves on Diane's blood.

"What the fuck?" Byron yelled. Wrapping the blanket around his fist, he gripped the body of a bloodworm and jerked it away from Diane, leaving a circular wound the size of a silver dollar, and four bleeding puncture wounds. With Diane's blood oozing from its mouth, he tossed the creature into the surf and removed the other two bloodworms from her lifeless body.

Distraught with fear and overwhelmed with remorse, Byron sat down next to her head and stroked her chalk-white face. "Diane. Please hang on. The ambulance will be here soon."

FORENSIC CLUES

Willow was preparing a fruit salad dinner when her phone rang.

"Willow. This is Doctor Joe McMasters."

"Hey, Doc. What's up?"

"I've been nosing around, trying to find some information on suspicious deaths that may be related to what happened to Karen, you know, people who have died or been attacked by marine organisms while in or on the ocean. I've done some independent research of sorts, and believe I've discovered something much more...and I'm not trying to scare you, but..."

Willow interrupted. "Bill Knight told me how Karen died, but he wouldn't go into detail over the phone. Maybe someone or some entity doesn't want the world to know what is really happening in the North Pacific. Hell, it may be happening in every ocean."

"Conspiracy theories can be dangerous. Listen, I might have another important data point for you. A friend of mine, an ER intern at the Kailua Hospital told me about a strange incident. Two weeks ago, a twenty-five-year-old Caucasian female, a local woman named Diane Templeton, was admitted with multiple bites from some kind of marine creature. She and her boyfriend had been skinny-dipping in Hanauma Bay. She suffered from toxic shock and died before they could administer any treatment. My ER friend said he thought it might have been bloodworms, big ones because the bite marks were the size of silver dollars and there were fang marks in her flesh."

"That's a common denominator with large bloodworms. Their venom can trigger anaphylactic shock."

"That's where the story gets disconnected. My ER friend said he didn't think the men who came to take her body were from the coroner's office. Their coveralls had no identifying name or logo and they wore face masks and gloves. He was quite surprised. I called the coroner's office and they said they had no record of anyone by the name of Diane Templeton or a bloodworm attack."

"That's perplexing. Why the hell would the coroner's office cover up her death? Maybe the police are involved. Who knows? Anyway, thanks, Doc. I really appreciate you reaching out with this information."

"Good luck, Willow. And be careful."

****

Blake sat at the kitchen table, punching away at his laptop keyboard when Willow strutted into view.

"Hot Damn! Look at the heartbreaker in the polka-dot bikini," Blake shouted. "You look like one of those college girls on spring break. Why are you wearing that skimpy bikini?"

"I'm going to the beach. Wanna join me? I haven't worn this since we first met in Chuuk Island. I'm surprised it still fits."

"It fits you too perfectly. You're gonna turn a lot of heads dressed in that outfit. It brings back fond memories of our first time together. What's with the cooler?"

"I know it sounds ridiculous, but I'm going fishing at Hanauma Bay."

"There haven't been any fish in Hanauma Bay for years."

"Bloodworms, actually. Please don't laugh. This is serious business."

"Okay, I won't laugh. But bloodworms? I recall you told me about being stung by one when you were a teenager, but bloodworms aren't really on my diet," Blake snickered.

"We're not going to eat them, silly. I've got to catch one for my research. Come with me. I'll explain the details on the way, but first, we have to stop at the meat market. I need to pick up a rump roast."

"I thought we were going out for dinner?"

"It's bloodworm bait."

****

They stumbled down the steep roadway to the beach. Dressed in her bikini and a summer shawl, Willow carried the cooler and the rump roast while Blake ferried two beach chairs and towels.

"This spot is as good as any. Set the beach chairs on the dry sand above the berm. We'll watch the bait from there. I'll secure the rump roast on the wet sand where the waves roll up and kids build those dripping sand castles."

"I can't believe we're actually fishing for bloodworms. Promise me you'll never mention this to any of my staff. They'd think I'm insane," Blake growled.

After setting the bait, Willow and Blake sat impatiently in their beach chairs and monitored the rump roast for any signs of subterranean movement.

"If we're lucky to catch one of these slimy critters, don't try to remove it from the bait. Just toss the bundle in the cooler and shut the lid," Willow warned.

The amiable incoming waves encircled the bait causing it to roll up the wet sand a few inches. As the water ebbed, the bait tumbled back to its original location. This cycle continued for several minutes until Willow saw movement in the wet sand.

"Blake, I think we've got a visitor. Look, see. There it is, wiggling just below the surface a few inches to the right of the bait."

"Yeah, I see it."

With the patience and skill of a masterful fisherman, Willow readied her mind and body for the strike, visualizing the sequence of her attack, mentally counting the seconds as the bloodworm inched its way through the wet sand toward the bait.

"Grab the cooler and follow me." Willow leaped out of her chair and dashed to the bait with Blake a few feet behind. She stopped within reach of the bait and paused to gather her moxie. Suddenly, the bait began to shift upwards.

"He's locking onto the meat. Give it a few seconds to engage his fangs and begin sucking. We'll catch it by surprise," Willow mumbled.

Looking at Blake, she held up a closed fist while her lips formed the numbers one, two, and three. Seamlessly, she lunged for the bait, grasping it with both hands. With the power and speed of a home-run hitter, she snatched the bait and bloodworm from the wet sand and tossed the squirming mass into the cooler.

"Whistling wahoo! That was an awesome adrenaline rush." Willow discreetly opened the lid of the cooler. "He's still sucking on the meat. Let's wrap up this operation. I've got to get back to my lab with this specimen. Thanks for your help, Blake. I could not have done this without you."

"I love helping you, particularly when you're wearing that outfit," Blake chuckled. "What's your plan?"

"I'll perform a genomic DNA, confirm the species and try to determine the composition of the venom. There's no doubt in my mind this creature has some foreign DNA. I also need to compare his anatomy to that of his ancestors."

****

"Bill, this is Willow. I've got some news."

Bill hesitated, contemplating whether to end the call or listen to what Willow had to say. "What's the latest?"

"I got a call from Doctor Joe. He told me about a woman who died at Hanauma Bay while skinny-dipping with her boyfriend. She was admitted to the ER with multiple bites from some kind of marine creature. An intern friend of Doctor Joe witnessed the event and said he thought it might have been bloodworms, big ones, because of the large bite marks and the fact that he saw fang marks on her backside. The intern said she probably died from anaphylactic shock. I know all about bloodworms. I was bitten by one when I was a kid. It's painful and can be deadly if you're allergic. Out of curiosity, Doctor Joe called the coroner to inquire about the incident and get more information. They told him they had no record of Diane Templeton or any bloodworm incident."

"I'm not surprised. I mean it. There is a concerted effort by some adversaries to hide the truth. What we know must be very threatening for them to go to these extremes."

"Blake and I managed to capture a bloodworm from the same beach where Diane Templeton was attacked. I plan to conduct a genomic DNA and toxicology workup. If my instincts are right, I bet these creatures have some foreign DNA and maybe a super-charged venom."

"Willow, we both know you're onto something big - bigger and more frightening than anything we could have imagined in our worst nightmares. I'm torn between helping you and putting my life on the line, or pulling the plug and forgetting all about it."

"What about the UN, CDC, NOAA. For Chrissakes, Bill, it's just a fucking garbage patch." Willow's blood pressure spiked.

"Hey, take a deep breath and think about what you just suggested. Like all the other so-called international watchdogs, the UN is nothing more than a diplomatic venue for a gang of scientists, environmentalists, and animal-rights folks to spend a few days at an expensive resort, eating, drinking and bullshitting until they take a first-class flight home to tell their constituents they have solved the crisis and not to worry. Meanwhile, their plutocratic overlords laugh their way to the bank. The UN Global Development Plan of 2020 is a perfect example. This ostentatious declaration guaranteed the people of the world that marine pollution of all kinds would be eliminated by 2030. Two hundred countries signed this declaration. And what happened? It became worse, much worse. Besides squeezing most of the life out of our oceans, we are beginning to discover extremophiles that are able to live and breed in this toxic environment. I can think of several entities that might not want that information to be made public."

"I understand, Bill, I really do. It's so frustrating. And it is precisely this kind of duplicity that leads me to believe we're very close to a point of no return."

"I've got to go. Good luck, Willow."

Bloodworm fangs

CHAPTER 10

THE TRUTH IS IN THE DNA

It was three in the morning. A procession of foreboding impulses, anxieties, and troubling questions continued to race around Willow's head. She navigated her way to the kitchen and made herself a cup of coffee. Bill's message was clear. She and Blake might be in danger if she blew the whistle and publicly disclosed her findings. She could not make a decision until she completed her analysis of the bloodworm, and then summarized her extensive list of data.

With a half-full cup of coffee, she wandered back to the bedroom to get dressed.

"Where are you going?" Blake looked at his watch. "Hey, sweet pea. It's almost three-thirty in the morning."

"I've got to go to the lab and examine the bloodworm. I'll call you from the lab. What's on your agenda for today?"

"We're modifying some of the life support systems in the habitat. We need larger, more efficient scrubbers. How about joining me for lunch?"

"I'll call you from the lab." Willow bent over Blake and planted a warm, wet kiss on his lips. "I love you."

****

After putting on her lab coat, facemask, and rubber gloves, she covered her hands with a pair of gloves designed for handling venomous snakes. She then opened the cooler and checked the bloodworm for signs of life. Seeing none, she carefully grasped the worm and forcefully pulled its fangs from the meat.

Placing the slippery creature on the digital scale, she uttered the physical dimensions and weight. "Forty centimeters long, five centimeters wide, eight hundred and forty-four grams. This one is a big mother."

She maneuvered the annelid to expose the mouth. "There are four copper-colored fangs, evenly spaced in a circle around the perimeter of the jaws."

Using a pair of tweezers, she pulled back the tissue surrounding the fangs, fully aware they might contain lethal venom. "The fangs are approximately fifteen millimeters long from the tip to the venom sack."

Willow then prepared the bloodworm for genomic DNA testing and placed the sample in the sequencer.

****

Throughout the world, there are thousands of species of bloodworms, some as small as a few millimeters, with a few growing to several feet. They live and breed in the oceans, seas, and some freshwater environments. Smaller species are farm-raised as bait for sports fishermen.

With a lifespan of two to five years, these organisms reproduce only once - when the body of the female ruptures, millions of eggs will be instantly fertilized by a writhing swarm of males.

With a suction cup mouth and four venomous fangs, bloodworms are extremely well equipped to satisfy their bloodthirsty appetite. The lethality of their venom varies from a bee sting to a venomous snake bite.

As with most bloodworms, the venom may continue to evolve due to changes in their prey or environment. Their ability to modify their venom formula exemplifies the single most important theme in evolutionary convergence, where some venomous organisms independently transform their venom recipe in order to prey on increasingly larger or more diversified food sources.

Even small genetic changes can radically increase the potency of their venom. Their ever-changing venom is a witch's brew of many different toxins. Depending on their primary food source, some venom recipes can trigger intense pain and shock, while others may shut down the central nervous system, paralyze muscles, inhibit breathing, or cause massive internal bleeding. Once their fangs inject their venom into the victim, the mouth of the bloodworm remains locked into the flesh while they suck blood and bodily fluids down their throat.

****

"Have you discovered any new monsters this morning?" Blake asked facetiously as Willow jumped into the passenger seat of his car.

"The bloodworm specimen is *americana*. I've got the DNA test to prove it. But its DNA also contains some foreign molecules. There is no doubt it has mutated. The fangs were about ten millimeters longer and more robust than any other specimens in my database. But the most terrifying difference in this species is the toxicology of the poison. Blake, this creature has the most complex venom that has ever been documented, more toxic than the Australian western taipan, the deadliest snake in the world. This bad boy could kill an elephant with a single strike."

"Well, isn't that a fine kettle of fish. They're living under the beaches of Hawaii."

"Affirmative!"

"God Almighty! How could this be? How could these organisms change from an obscure pest to an aggressive killing machine?"

"They adapted by genetic mutation. Their ancestors survived the Cambrian extinction five hundred million years ago, the Jurassic a hundred and fifty million years ago, and many other extinction events including asteroid and meteor impacts and huge volcanic eruptions that wiped out most of the living organisms of the planet. That's why they are called extremophiles."

"Are humans extremophiles?" Blake inquired optimistically.

"That's a great question. Maybe. Maybe not. The fact is, we don't know. Humans are complex organisms with great power over our environment and the world we occupy. From an evolutionary point of view, we've come a long way in a relatively short period of time. But we don't always have the ability to control our emotions or behavior or adapt our bodies or metabolism to rapidly changing environmental conditions. If it's freezing outside, we put on a coat. If it's too hot, we turn on the air conditioner and jump in the pool. And if there is no food to buy or steal, we starve. The animals we're dealing with, these true extremophiles, are simple organisms. They don't have a brain, they can't change their clothes, they can kill and eat just about anything and they don't need to mate to reproduce."

"Maybe that's the problem. We humans like to make whoopie," Blake snickered.

"Yeah, maybe all that kissin' and a-humpin' might be a big part of the problem. One thing is certain, at least in my mind, this planet is incapable of supporting ten billion human souls. And if these primitive extremophiles continue to mutate, they may one day win the battle over us humans and survive the next extinction event."

"Extinction! Christ Almighty, Willow. You don't really mean that, do you?"

"Another great question, Blake. Let's break it down into the basic elements for sustaining human life. First is water. Humans cannot live more than a few days without it. Second is food. Healthy humans can go a couple of weeks or more without food. Starving people will not survive more than a few days."

"So, without water or food, we'll all be gone in less than a month?"

"Probably, except for those who can buy or steal increasingly more expensive drinking water and food. Here's something you may not know. It takes two gallons of water to put a gallon of water in a plastic jug and deliver it to the consumer."

"That's outrageous. What are some of the other possibilities?"

"There are several, with vastly different trajectories. Human avarice is the primary cause of things like the Great Pacific Garbage Patch. In case you didn't know, one of the biggest contributors to the garbage patch is the friendly bottled water company. Over the past fifty years, they've spent hundreds of millions indoctrinating their customers into believing bottled water is good and tap water is bad. Their marketing strategy worked and now nets these companies billions of dollars a year."

"I get it, consumer propaganda. Advertising. If our tap water is so damn unhealthy why not filter it at the faucet?"

"That is precisely my point. Today, the seas can no longer feed us, so we use some of our agricultural lands to grow fish food for fish farms. Those who can afford to eat farm-raised fish can buy it. But the fish food, the wheat and grains that are fed to the fish, could also feed starving people."

"I don't like the taste of farmed fish. It's got an unnatural chemical tang."

"As the fight for fresh water and food escalates, we can expect more outbreaks of civil unrest in Africa, India, and the Middle East. In fact, we're witnessing this as we speak. Of course, this could also occur in the United States and more advanced countries as well. Only the rich will survive. There's also the possibility of a virulent biological outbreak, a pandemic explosion, where wealth, power, and social status are irrelevant. And if that doesn't do us in, there are asteroids, meteors, polar shift, nuclear holocaust, and an invasion of the body snatchers from outer space." Willow and Blake chuckled at her reference to body snatchers.

"As apocalyptic as it sounds, there must be something we can do. What can you and I do as private citizens? How do we win the battle?"

"We've got to keep the faith and continue to be optimistic. Somehow we need to convince the oligarchs, the people who really run the world, Bilderberg Group, Council of Foreign Relations, the uber-rich and powerful, to think the same way as ordinary people." Willow had a knack for bringing complex issues into focus.

"As much as I love you, and admire you, and trust you, I don't believe you or anyone else is omnipotent."

"Listen, Blake. I love you dearly and I would never do anything to hurt you, but I've been thinking about disclosing my work to Simeon Jaegger. He's the Director of the Marine Resources Commission at the United Nations. He's the only person I know who might listen. He knows some very wealthy people, power brokers, lobbyists, and politicians. Maybe he can help."

CHAPTER 11

BUGS AT SEA

He had first seen her in the Gould School of Law library. She was bent over a digital reader with a bottle of water in her free hand. He knew the librarian well enough to ascertain her name and was determined to meet her.

A few days later, he saw her drinking her morning coffee with a couple of her fellow law school students in an overcrowded West 36th Street coffee shop. Michael couldn't stop staring at the voluptuous blonde wearing a pair of blue summer shorts, leather sandals, and a white cotton shirt emblazoned with the gold letters USC. She could have been the poster girl for a USC recruiting poster - the perfect image of a California surfer girl.

"Come on man. Be bold!" The words came from a voice in his head.

"Okay," he mumbled and briskly walked up to her like a colonel addressing his troops.

"Hi, my name is Michael."

"Hi, Michael. I'm Skyler. Do I know you?" Mildly amused at his bravado, her two friends began to giggle.

"Nope. We've never met. I just couldn't help myself. You're so beautiful."

Annoyed at her snickering friends, she raised her head shamelessly and barked at their juvenile behavior. "What?"

Turning back to Michael, she smiled. "Thank you, Michael. I think I've seen you before. Gould library, maybe?"

"Yup. That was me. Would you like to take a ride on my sailboat?"

"Now?"

"Now would be great."

"Where's your boat?"

"Marina Del Rey. *Lady Love*. Cal 24."

"*Lady Love*. Are you serious?"

"Why not? It beats bar hopping."

"Sure, why not, as long as we're back before dark. I've got a final tomorrow."

She picked up her belongings and faced her friends. "If I'm not back in time for the final, call the cops."

****

Michael and Skyler had grown up in Newport Beach. While an undergrad at USC, Michael took full advantage of his muscular six-foot-three frame by excelling as a competitive swimmer. As a junior, he won the hundred-yard freestyle sprint at the Pac 12 Championships, helping USC win the league trophy.

Since high school, Skyler had played competitive beach volleyball. While an undergrad, she and her partner narrowly missed qualifying for the 1996 Olympic Games in Atlanta. Since the widely televised Olympic trials, she and her teammate spent many weekends taking on challengers at the Venice and Marina Del Rey beaches.

Michael and Skyler were meant for each other. It was love and lust at first sight - an exuberant and rapturous relationship. Three weeks after their first rendezvous on his *Lady Love* sailboat, they moved into a small apartment and continued to work toward their law degrees. After they both passed the bar, they married and moved to San Diego to start their own legal practice.

As their law practice grew, so did their family. Skyler gave birth to two sons, Jason, now thirty-three, and Daniel, twenty-eight. To their friends and relatives, the Michael and Skyler Brady family provided an iconic portrait of a happy and prosperous family.

San Diego provided the perfect backdrop for sailing, be it on the bay, off the west coast of America or in the Sea of Cortez. Now, after almost four decades of sailing experience, they decided it was time to take on a greater sailing challenge - a voyage to Hawaii.

****

"Cast off her bowline," Michael shouted to his eldest son, Jason.

"Aye, aye skipper." Jason cast off the line and leaped aboard *Justice* from the Harbor Island Marina docks.

Having sailed hundreds of times with his parents, from day trips on the bay to weeklong voyages along the west coast, Jason was well qualified to pilot and navigate the vessel when his father or mother needed a break.

"Can we help?" Jason's wife Lisa asked, holding the hand of their thirteen-year-old daughter, Tara.

"There's not much to do while we motor out. Just enjoy the scenery. There'll be lots of chores later." Michael swung the helm of his Mason 40 to starboard, minimizing the wake of an oncoming naval vessel.

"We'll motor past the breakwater. Then set the sails. Hawaii, here we come!"

"What a fabulous June day. It's perfect for sailing. I wish Daniel could be with us. He'd go bananas. But duty calls. I hope he's enjoying Pensacola and his naval aviation assignment," Skyler said, handing Michael a hot cup of freshly brewed coffee. "What's the weather forecast?"

"The three-day forecast is for two- to four-foot seas, partly cloudy skies, and ten- to fifteen-knot winds."

After taking a sip of his coffee, he gave Sky a peck on the cheek. "As soon as we clear the point, we'll head southwest for a couple of days and then turn northwest to capture the prevailing wind. With any luck, we'll have the wind at our backs for most of the journey. I reckon we'll be at sea for sixteen to twenty days." Michael chuckled as the wind ruffled his thick grey hair. "That's a nice hat you're wearing, sweetie."

"I bought it especially for this trip." Skyler grabbed the brim as a gust of wind threatened to steal it from her.

"You probably should keep it tied under your chin."

Justice was the perfect ocean-going sailboat and the envy of every sailor in the San Diego Yacht Club. Her hull was painted a metallic pearl white surrounded by a dark blue banner painted below her gunnel. She was a sleek vessel with exceptional stability and steerage. Most importantly, her main and headsail were motorized for automatic furling.

When it came to communications, Michael equipped *Justice* with the most advanced marine-grade hardware available, including GPS-driven auto-pilot, a Sea Link, 2Mb IP network providing high-speed Internet, streaming video, email with large file attachments, voice calls, and text messaging.

The cabin design was spacious and well suited for family cruising. Hand-polished teak and brass hardware dominated the interior. Berthing included three double-size cabins. The saloon and galley were separated by a teakwood bar and the comm center.

Bulletproof is the word to best describe the construction of *Justice*. The solid fiberglass hull was an inch thick at the top of the keel. The lead ballast was encapsulated in the keel, capable of withstanding a head-on collision with a coral head or a migrating humpback whale without puncturing the hull.

Sailing the wild ocean on *Justice* was easy on the body and soothing to the soul. Michael, Skyler, and Jason divided the day into six, four-hour shifts. Every other day they exchanged positions in the rotation. Lisa and Tara prepared the meals and kept the interior in tip-top shape.

****

Justice was six days into her voyage when Jason called out, "Humpbacks off the starboard bow!" As *Justice* closed the gap, Michael joined Jason and they both watched a mother humpback and her calf struggling to keep up with the rest of her traveling companions.

"Look, there's a pod of killer whales," Michael said, pointing to the pod of black and white cetaceans. "They're splitting into two groups. There's a big male and a few smaller males and females in each group. Jason, see their black and white coloring? It's different on each animal, making it easy for the other orcas to identify each one of them. I think the orcas are on the hunt. Humpback whales are one of their prime targets. This could get bloody. You may want to go below."

"I'll watch. I know Mother Nature can be brutal."

Michael and Jason continued to observe the hunt, knowing from watching numerous Wild Kingdom documentaries that it would shortly turn into a brutal, one-sided battle.

****

Healthy adult humpback whales reach fifty feet in length and weigh about seventy thousand pounds. They have a distinctive body shape, with long pectoral fins and a lumpy head. They are easily recognized for their breaching - leaping high above the water, and then crashing back into the sea with a glorious gush of foaming whitewater.

Whales are air-breathing mammals and must surface to breathe in fresh air. They migrate up to fifteen thousand miles each year, traveling from polar waters to subtropical waters to breed and give birth.

What remains of a once large humpback population still migrates to the Hawaiian Islands every winter. They feed primarily in summer and live off fat reserves during winter. They are energetic hunters, taking krill and small schooling fish such as juvenile salmon, mackerel, anchovies, and sardines.

Like other large whales, at one time the humpback was a high-value revenue source for the whaling industry. Hunted to the brink of extinction, their population fell by ninety-five percent before the world took protective action. Despite all the demagoguery and promises about saving these magnificent animals, entanglement in fishing gear, collisions with ships, pollution, and killer whale predation continued to devastate the ever-shrinking population beyond the possibility of recovery.

****

As the orcas prepared to execute their attack plan, the humpback mother emitted a long, high-pitched moan - a sorrowful cry to her nearby pod that could be heard across the sea for miles.

Led by the largest male, the first group of orcas dove under the mother humpback, and then quickly surfaced between her and her three-ton calf. Their strategy was obvious - to separate the mother from the baby.

The mother quickly repositioned herself between the attackers and her baby while the second group of orcas repeated the separation maneuver - driving a wedge between mother and baby. The mother pushed her calf with her head, encouraging him to swim faster than the attackers.

Relentlessly, the first squad of orcas repeated the separation maneuver followed immediately by the second squad. Each time the orcas attacked, the humpback mother managed to resume her protective position. However, the infant was slowly depleting his strength and his breathing became increasingly labored. Likewise, over the next several minutes, the mother humpback gradually lost her ability to protect her offspring from the onslaught. The orcas sensed the victory was at hand and went for the kill.

"I can't watch this anymore. It's too gruesome. I'm going below." Jason returned to the cabin to comfort Lisa and their daughter. Michael remained topside, piloting *Justice* and witnessing the butchery.

The end came like a high-speed train wreck. The big males dove deep, and then rushed to the surface as a group, delivering a mighty blow to the infant's head and abdomen, knocking the wind from its lungs and disorienting its senses. The dominant male raced forward, snapped his long conical teeth on the infant's lower jaw, exposing its tongue. With humpback blood tainting the surrounding water, the remaining orcas rushed in and out of the gaping mouth, ripping off large chunks of the infant's tongue.

But the carnage was not over. The orcas sensed the mother's exhaustion and repeatedly attacked until she could no longer fight back. The moment she opened her mouth, the killers began biting off bucket-size portions of her tongue. Bleeding profusely, both mother and baby slowly expired, rolled belly-up and became fodder for roaming sharks.

Apparently satiated, the orcas retreated. A few of them celebrated their feast by catapulting their massive bodies several feet out of the water, then falling back to the ocean, sending an immense cascade of water high into the air.

The orcas departed as a group, leaving a blood-stained spume the size of a soccer field and two mutilated humpbacks drifting on the surface of the ocean.

****

"Good morning, pop. It's gonna be a hot day." Jason passed his father a hot cup of coffee and sat next to him near the helm.

"Thanks, son," Michael said while exploring the horizon. "That was a disturbing scene yesterday. My God, those killer whales were ferocious."

"Survival of the fittest. It's much more dramatic in real life than in a Wild Kingdom documentary. I couldn't watch the end. I knew how it was going to end."

"The sharks had a quite a feast too. Maybe the killer whales and sharks have a symbiotic relationship."

"What's our location, Pop?"

"About six hundred miles east of Hilo. If we don't get some wind, it'll be another week or so until we reach port."

"Have you noticed how the sun always seems larger when you're sailing in the open sea?"

"Yeah, even bigger when it's flat."

"We're not making much headway, are we?" Jason asked.

"No. Not in these doldrums. I've been out here since four this morning. I can't believe all the garbage. It's everywhere - millions of tons of human waste as far as I can see." Michael waved his arm in a wide arc. "There are plastic bottles everywhere. You'd think someone would build an ocean-going trash collector. It might be a very profitable recycling operation. Look, Jason. There's a dead turtle tangled in a garbage bag. Poor thing. If I had known it was going to be this bad, I'd have opted for a trip to Tahiti."

"Don't fret, Dad. None of us had a clue this was so massive."

"Ouch! Goddamn gnats." Michael swatted his bare arm leaving a large red welt as retribution. "These little bastards are everywhere. They're pesky little critters and sting like mosquitoes. I've been whacking them since before sunup. I covered myself with bug repellent. It didn't have much effect."

"Yikes! One just nailed me too. Shit, Dad. Bugs at sea? Ouch! There goes another one. Son of a bitch. He stabbed me in the arm. Look, that little bastard drew blood. These things really hurt. Look at the welt on my arm. It itches like crazy too."

"Maybe they're a cousin of the New Zealand blackfly. Your mother and I experienced those nasty bloodsuckers in Milford Sound. It's spectacular scenery, one of God's treasures. Why he chose to put a vampire fly into such a pristine place of beauty is beyond my comprehension. They look like gnats, swarm like locusts, and bite like hell. I recall large clouds of these ravenous insects attacking us out of nowhere, buzzing in and out of our ears, noses, and even our mouths. Your mother and I spent most of the time swatting and swearing. Bug spray was useless. And their bite was just as painful as these tiny bastards."

"I'm going back to our cabin and put on a long-sleeved shirt and pants. It's my watch and I don't fancy being a pincushion for the next four hours." Jason hurriedly went below.

"Tell the girls to put on long-sleeved shirts and pants if they want to come topside. Better yet, have them stay below," Michael yelled as Jason descended into the saloon.

Moments later, Jason returned to commence his eight-to-noon watch while Michael went below to eat some breakfast and take a nap.

"Michael, what's happened to your face? Are those bug bites?"

"Yeah. Remember those nasty blackfly's in Milford Sound. Well, these are just as aggressive and more painful. Do we have any cortisone cream?"

"It's in the medical kit. I'll get it. You sit and try to enjoy your coffee."

****

The bugs must have sensed Jason was fresh meat and as the sun climbed higher in the sky, they picked up the pace of their attacks. He did his best to shield his flesh from the painful bites, but they were tenacious devils and a few managed to find a sweet spot of warm flesh under his protective clothing where they could insert their blood-sucking proboscis.

After an hour of standing watch and several dozen bites, the tormentors had succeeded in creating numerous puffy red welts on Jason's head and hands. The itching became intolerable and he began to feel the shocking effects of what he believed to be an allergic reaction. Finding it increasingly difficult to breathe, Jason stumbled back to the saloon.

Skyler immediately jumped to assist her son. "Jason, my poor baby." Skyler was horrified. "Your face is puffed up like a basketball. And your hands - they're swollen and red. Quick, come and lie down on the sofa. I'll see if we have any epinephrine."

"It itches like crazy, Mom." Jason wheezed with each labored breath. "It feels like a bee sting only much worse. I feel woozy. Everything looks out of focus."

"Do we have any epinephrine?" Skyler shouted. "Jason is having a reaction to these bugs."

"I think there is some in the medical cabinet. I'll get it."

Michael handed Skyler a few auto-injectors and she immediately administered one to Jason's thigh.

"That should make you feel better," Sky whispered. "I'll get a wet towel to cover your mouth and nose. Maybe that will help your breathing."

Michael bent over and patted Jason on the forehead. "You take it easy, son. Just relax. The symptoms should subside in a while. In the meantime, I'll take the watch."

"No, Dad. I can handle it. Just give me a few minutes."

"Nonsense. We're a family and you need to stay put, young man. Let Mom do her thing. She's taken good care of you since you were born."

"No, Dad. Listen. The bugs are everywhere. They stick in your eyes. You can't even breathe."

"You rest. Stay on the sofa. I'll take the watch." Michael grabbed a towel and covered his head like a nomadic camel herder wandering about the Sahara Desert.

The instant Michael stepped onto the main deck, the bloodthirsty insects furiously attacked. Hundreds of them swarmed around his head and shoulders. Several converged around his eyes. Within seconds, a few had pierced his flesh and begun siphoning his blood through their built-in straw. Realizing he was no match for the overwhelming invasion, he dashed back into the sanctuary of the saloon.

"It's impossible to stand watch. The insects are everywhere - thousands of them. They're swarming like locusts. I must have killed hundreds of them, eight or ten with a single swat. But no matter what I did to cover up, there were just too many of them. Look, I've got bites on my face, eyes, and hands. They even stung me through my shirt. Jesus Christ, I look like a pomegranate. How's Jason?"

"He's not well," Skyler replied. "He's having trouble breathing. The epinephrine didn't have any effect. I don't think he's suffering an allergic reaction. These are not bee stings. These bites are from a different insect. Do you know what they are? I sure don't. We know nothing about them." Skyler's face transmuted to the look of a grieving widow.

"Come, Michael, let me help you to our cabin. You need to get horizontal - try to get some sleep. I'll rub some cortisone ointment on your sores."

"What else can we do?" Lisa wiped the sweat from Jason's forehead with the wet towel.

"As soon as Michael is in bed, I'll check the Internet. There must be some information on the mariners' websites."

****

After a two-hour Internet search using every possible keyword, Skyler was still searching for answers. Running out of options, she decided to call the family doctor in San Diego.

"Scripps Medical," greeted the receptionist.

"This is Skyler Brady. I have an urgent situation. I'm calling from the middle of the Pacific Ocean. I need to speak with Doctor Webber."

"Hi, Mrs. Brady. Let me check."

Moments later Doctor Webber answered the call.

"Hello, Sky. My receptionist said you were calling from the middle of the ocean. What can I do to help?"

"Michael and I, we're on our sailboat with Jason and his wife and daughter. We're about six hundred miles from Hilo. Michael and Jason have been attacked by some stinging bugs. I have no idea what they are, but both men are suffering terrible reactions. Their faces are swollen, they're having trouble breathing, and the bites are inflamed. It's much worse than bee stings - even Africanized bees don't do this."

"Do you have any epinephrine?"

"Yes, but it didn't have any effect. We don't know what to do. We're stuck out here. We're heading for Hilo, but we won't arrive for several days. I'm concerned we may not make it in time."

"Send me some photos. It might be a bacterial or viral infection. I'll discuss it with our infectious disease specialist and get back to you."

"Thank you. Please hurry."

"I presume you don't have any antibiotics?"

"No, we don't have anything like that. Hurry!"

****

"Let's get a drink in the bar and talk about this," Skyler said, taking Lisa by the hand.

"Yeah, I need a drink."

Sky walked across the saloon to the bar where she found a bottle of Scotch whiskey and poured a double. "What can I get you?"

"Something strong. Whatever you're drinking is okay."

"How are we going to get out of this mess?" Skyler whispered. "We're not equipped to handle this kind of emergency. Our husbands need professional medical treatment."

Lisa took a sip of her drink.

Frustrated at not being able to diagnose the affliction, Sky promptly gulped down the entire contents of her glass in three successive swallows.

"Maybe the weather will pick up and they'll go away?" Sky said with a breath of wishful thinking.

"I hope so. Jason is really sick and he's getting worse," Lisa whimpered through quivering lips.

"I don't know what we can do except pray. Christ Almighty! We're hundreds of miles from Hilo."

Looking at each other with the somber expressions of coffin bearers, Skyler wrapped her arms around Lisa and, feeling her racing heartbeat, gave her a compassionate hug.

"Maybe we should have stayed home?" Lisa muttered.

"We've been through some formidable times in the past. One way or another, we'll get through this one too." Skyler flashed an optimistic smile.

Lisa returned to the saloon to check on Jason. Tracing her fingers across Jason's forehead she bellowed, "God, you're burning up.

Jason, please talk to me. Jason, say something. You're really scaring me. Please talk to me."

"What? Where am I?" Jason murmured in a raspy voice. "Have we arrived in Hilo?"

"No, honey. We've got a few more days. You just rest. Everything will be fine."

Lisa hurriedly retrieved a thermometer from the medical kit and placed it under Jason's tongue.

"How's he doing?" Sky asked.

With her eyes bubbling with newborn tears, Lisa gave her a disheartening expression. "He's a hundred and three. I tried to get him to talk but he's not coherent."

****

It was after midnight when Michael was awakened by a painful jolt racing up his spine, across his chest and into his head. He tried to get out of bed, but his equilibrium faltered, causing him to quickly drop to the floor. Dazed, he placed the back of his hand over his forehead and wiped away a river of perspiration. Engulfed in a spinning world of vertigo, Michael curled up in anguish.

"Sky! Help!" Michael cried out, struggling to stand up.

Skyler jumped out of bed and rushed to his side, shuddering at the sight of Michael's condition.

"Oh, hell. You look ghastly."

"I'm sick. I ache all over. Feel my head. I'm on fire."

Skyler felt his forehead. "You have a fever. I'll get some cold water. Let me help you back to bed."

Skyler felt helpless, befuddled as to the cause of the affliction.

"Oh, baby. It hurts so bad. Get me something. Oxycodone. Anything." Michael fell back onto the bed."

"Lisa," Sky called out. "Can you get me some pain meds? Michael is sick."

There was no answer.

"Hang on, honey. I'll be right back." Michael pressed the towel to his forehead.

Skyler rushed to the saloon and found Lisa sitting on the floor, her eyes transfixed on Jason - numerous oozing ulcers littered his swollen face, hands, and arms.

Lisa cried out. "Look at his face. It's horrible. It's getting worse. He's got some on his neck and chest too. They're getting deeper and bigger. Oh, God. What's happening?"

"Lisa, Lisa." Skyler shook her by the shoulders. "Lisa, look at me! Michael is sick - the same as Jason. I'll help you to your cabin. Tara is waiting. She needs you."

"But Jason needs me. He's really sick. He needs my help. He's not going to die, is he?"

"No, no. He's going to be okay. There's nothing you can do. Come, Tara needs you."

Skyler took Lisa by the arm and escorted her to her cabin. As soon as Skyler opened the cabin door, Tara dashed to her mother and buried her head against her shoulder.

"Where have you been? Where's daddy?"

"Daddy is very sick." Lisa wrapped her arms around Tara and held her close while biting her lower lip.

****

Skyler gathered up her strength, found some pain meds and returned to her cabin. Michael remained exactly as she had left him. Taking a closer look at his face, she instantly lurched back. Several ulcerated sores had appeared down his neck, cheek, and temples. Michael coaxed a muffled moan from his throat and slowly turned to face his wife.

"Michael," Skyler cooed. "Open your mouth. Let me take your temperature."

Michael didn't move.

"Michael. It's me, Sky. Open your mouth. I need to take your temperature."

Without opening his eyes, he let his lower jaw drop.

"Oh, Jesus. Look at your mouth. It's covered with weeping sores. And your face and arms, my God, you're covered with bloody ulcers. God, what the hell is happening?"

Moments later she removed the thermometer from Michael's mouth.

"One hundred and five!" she exclaimed. "No, that can't be right."

"Michael, my dear Michael. I love you with all my heart. I will always love you. Don't you dare leave me."

Unable to reply, Michael exhaled a collection of unintelligible words, each one wrapped in spittle dripping from the corner of his mouth. With his eyes frozen in time, he coerced a smirk.

****

Skyler leaped at the first ring tone from the comm center.

"Hello, Mrs. Brady. This is Doctor Abernathy. Doctor Webber told me about your husband and son. What is their present condition?"

"Both of them are delirious. Oozing ulcers have erupted over their entire bodies. It's the most gruesome thing I could ever imagine."

"Take some photos and send them to me at scrippsabernathy dot com. I cannot make any diagnosis based on what you and Doctor Webber have told me. I'm sorry, but I need more information."

"I'll send the photos immediately."

****

Michael's condition vacillated from an immobile coma to shivering convulsions.

Sky quietly entered their cabin to check on his condition. With his mouth partially open she inserted the thermometer and let a heartfelt prayer glide across her thoughts.

Sky knew enough about medical symptoms to conclude Michael and Jason were suffering from a rare, perhaps unknown, infection. But the most shocking and puzzling symptom was the explosive appearance of oozing ulcers consuming the flesh of her husband and son.

Unable to sleep, Sky spent several hours walking the length of the central passage from their cabin to the saloon. Each time she passed the comm center she paused and exhaled a deep breath, envisaging Doctor Abernathy's call.

Her vigilant walkathon suddenly ceased with the sound of a ringtone from the comm center. It had been twenty-four hours since she had emailed the photos of Michael and Jason to Doctor Abernathy.

"Hello," Skyler nervously answered.

"Mrs. Brady. This is Doctor Abernathy." He paused long enough for Sky to prognosticate his message.

"Yes, Doctor. What can you tell me about my son and husband?"

"I wish I had better news, but I've exhausted all my resources. I've talked to several of my colleagues and we're…I'm not proud to say this, but we're stumped. It could be any number of things. High on our list is a mutated form of strep or staph, or perhaps MSRA. New strains of these bacteria have been known to emerge very quickly based on a number of factors. The only chance of killing these organisms is massive doses of a broad-spectrum antibiotic, and that is not always successful, particularly after the first twenty-four hours. I'm sorry, but there is nothing we can do. I suggest you call in the Coast Guard. Use your emergency beacon."

****

It was well past midnight when Sky awoke. *Justice* rocked from port to starboard in a gentle breeze. Moonbeams poured through the starboard portholes painting the interior of the cabin with a shadowy glow.

Michael's head rested heavily on his pillow. She carefully maneuvered out of bed and pulled a blanket over his breathless body.

Plodding barefoot toward the saloon, she was not surprised to see Lisa seated on the floor, holding Jason's cold hand. Lisa looked up at Sky, and then kissed Jason's hand. Rising to her feet, she took the blanket and reverently covered Jason's body.

"I'll miss him forever. He was a wonderful man, a loving husband, and a great father," Lisa mumbled.

"Where's Tara?" Sky asked.

"She's sleeping in our cabin. She knows what's happening."

Unable to hold back their anguish, the two women hugged each other and began to sob.

Wiping away her tears, Skyler regained some of her composure. "Come, Lisa. We need to seal the boat. Let's get some towels, rags, anything to block the seams and cracks in the hatchways, windows, and vents. Cover and lock all the points of entry. We're not going to let any of those fucking devils into our boat."

CHAPTER 12

FAKE NEWS

Seated at the kitchen table preparing a marine biology test, Willow pecked away at her laptop keyboard with her right index finger while sipping a lukewarm cup of her strongest Kona coffee. Blake intercepted her concentration when he sounded off from their family room.

"Hey, Willow. Check out CNN. There's a newsflash about a sailboat that foundered off the coast of Hilo. The Coast Guard reported two adult women and a young girl were the only survivors. The women told the authorities their husbands caught a couple of pufferfish and decided to eat them. The coroner said they probably died from tetrodotoxin poisoning because they didn't clean the fish."

Willow rushed to the living room but was too late to catch the full story. "Did they say pufferfish?"

"Yeah. They also said the surviving women were under investigation for possible foul play. The deceased husbands were wealthy lawyers. There's some big insurance money at stake."

"That's impossible. The coroner must be mistaken. Pufferfish are found in coastal waters, not offshore. And every yachtsman knows pufferfish can be deadly. Nobody in their right mind would eat one, except filthy-rich Japanese snobs. Chefs spend three years in training before they can legally prepare what they call *fugu*. The puffer is the most poisonous fish in the world. The active toxin, tetrodotoxin, paralyzes the diaphragm muscles and the victim dies from suffocation."

"Baby, you're preaching to the choir."

"Sorry, honey. Sometimes I get a bit carried away."

Driven by her suspicious instincts, Willow returned to the kitchen and called the Hilo Coroner's Office.

****

"Hilo Coroner's Office. How may I direct your call?" the operator said with a Pidgin English twist.

"I would like to speak with Doctor Jeffery Sakashita, please." Willow knew she'd have trouble controlling herself when mentioning his name and pinched her lower lip to contain her laughter.

"May I say who is calling?"

"Doctor Willow Parker."

"One moment please."

After two rings, the coroner answered his phone.

"This is Sakashita." Willow almost lost it.

"Hello, Jeff. This is Willow Parker, from the university."

"Doctor Parker. How nice to hear from you. How's everything? I watched your podcast on the Great Pacific Garbage Patch. It was impressive. I don't agree with everything you suggested, but you never know. Mother Nature works in mysterious ways. What can I do for you?"

"Blake saw a piece on television about some folks on a sailboat who allegedly died from tetrodotoxin poisoning after eating pufferfish. I assume your office provided the details of the autopsy. I wanted to speak with you personally regarding your findings."

"And your point is?" Sakashita's sharp words were far less hospitable than his greeting.

"First, you and I both know there are no pufferfish in the offshore waters of Hawaii. Second, I have to believe these men knew that fugu could kill them."

"And your point is?"

A five-year-old could have sensed his deception.

"My point is your office issued an erroneous statement."

"It's my office, and I stand by the official statement. Surely you understand. Some things are not as they appear. Some things are meant to sustain the status quo. Do you catch my drift?"

"How could you make a blatantly false report? Where's your honor and integrity? Why would you do such an irresponsible thing?"

"I'm sorry. I've got to go. Someday you may understand. Goodbye."

"Good grief. That was awkward." Perplexed, Willow glanced at Blake and scowled.

Blake overheard Willow's part of the conversation. "What did the friendly coroner tell you?"

"For starters, he wasn't very friendly. He basically told me to fuck off. That's not like the doctor I knew from our earlier days."

"Knowing you as I do, you're not about to let this thing go. So what's your next move?"

"Visit the Coast Guard station. Inspect the sailboat. Snoop around. You're right about me, my dear Blake. I am tenacious."

****

"Hilo Coast Guard. Sergeant Higgins speaking."

"Hello, Sergeant Higgins. My name is Doctor Parker. I'm a professor at the University of Hawaii in Waimanalo. I understand you have a sailboat impounded at your station. The university is interested in buying it. I've been asked to give them a report on its condition. Would it be possible to speak with the owner, the widow of the deceased?"

"I believe Mrs. Brady, her daughter-in-law, and granddaughter returned to San Diego right after the funeral."

"When was the funeral?"

"Three, maybe four weeks ago."

"But I just heard about the accident yesterday on CNN?"

"Yeah. That doesn't surprise me. It was pretty crazy around here for several days. Guys running around in suits and ties - some wore white hazmat suits. They musta been onto something fishy. They had two guards on the pier twenty-four-seven. The press wanted to take some pictures and interview the survivors, but they wouldn't let anyone near the boat. Then one day, they all packed up and left. A clean-up crew showed up the next day and scrubbed down the deck and sanitized the interior. I understand it was pretty grotesque, two dead bodies, five or six days at sea. Phew! I'm surprised the survivors didn't wrap them up and toss them into the sea."

"Would it be possible for me to make a quick walk-through inspection? I have a security clearance from the university."

"Hold on a second. Let me check with the duty officer." Minutes later, Higgins returned to their conversation.

"How soon can you get here?"

"I'll be at the base shortly after lunch. Please make out a guest pass and clear my name through security."

"No problem. Ask for Sergeant Arnold. He's got the next watch."

****

The flight from Honolulu to Hilo took less than an hour. Like a Sherlock Holmes wannabe, Willow had packed a small backpack with a few lab supplies just in case she found something of interest.

The taxi driver dropped her off at the Hilo Coast Guard station security gate where she received her name tag and a map of the facility. Aside from two Coast Guard cutters, the sloop *Justice* was the only vessel moored to the pier.

While she checked in with Sergeant Arnold, he advised her that the interior of *Justice* was locked because the police had not yet finished their work inside the cabin. Her inspection would be limited to the exterior of the vessel.

From the foot of the pier, the sloop looked just like any other rich man's toy - sleek, powerful, fast, and flirtatious. Emblazoned on the stern in bold cursive letters was her name: *Justice*. Below the name, the words *San Diego* signified her home port. Willow retrieved her smartphone and snapped a couple of pictures of the stern, then walked toward the bow while taking random snapshots along the starboard side. When she reached the bow, she took a few images of the registration number.

There was no evidence of a collision from her waterline to gunnels, a distance of about eight feet. Her flanks were sparkling clean as if they'd been washed and polished for the Admiral's inspection. The sails and rigging were neatly secured. She sure didn't look like she'd been at sea for a month. Rather, she appeared ready to show to prospective buyers. Willow thought the pristine condition of the vessel was peculiar.

The gangway from the pier to the main deck slowly oscillated up and down with each passing swell, but the guardrail allowed a safe passage over the water to the main deck.

Willow turned to face the bow and focused her intuitive senses on the deck. The starboard deck glistened, casting sharp reflections of the sun into her eyes. As she rounded the bow, she examined the anchor winch. Just forward of the winch was a small hatchway that led to the anchor chain storage locker.

She opened the hatch cover and, as expected, found a coil of heavy nylon rope filling most of the locker. As she raised herself upright, her eyes captured the shape of a dark fibrous substance, similar to a clump of hair, trapped in a narrow gap where the lip of the hatch cover seated against a rubber gasket. After snapping on a pair of rubber gloves, she pinched the substance between her thumb and index finger, placed it in a sterile container and put it in her backpack.

Finding nothing of interest on the port side, she returned to the exit.

"Thanks, Sergeant. Do you know whom I should contact regarding the interior?"

"Hilo PD. Like I said, they placed the padlock on the cabin door."

CHAPTER 13

HALOBATES - AGENTS OF PESTILENCE

Upon arriving at the Honolulu airport, Willow raced through the terminal to the sidewalk taxi kiosk.

"Waimanalo. Makai pier!" she ordered the driver. Beads of perspiration trickled from her forehead as the driver steered his Prius onto Interstate H-1. Passing Diamond Head, she called Blake.

"Hey, it's me. I'm back. I can't talk now, but I need you to clear out anyone using the Makai lab. I've got something I need to work on immediately."

"Sure, honey. I understand. Is there anything else I can do?"

"Cancel my afternoon class and don't let anyone know I'm back. Make up some excuse. Be sure to lock the door to the lab. I'm going to be working late and cannot be disturbed."

"As you often say, Jumpin' jellyfish. You must be on to something big."

"I can't get into that now, but it's very - how shall I put it - interesting. What have you been up to?"

"I'm glad you asked. I had a couple of spooky visitors show up at the pier this morning. They identified themselves as FBI agents. They had a federal warrant for all the images, videos, and reports related to the Karen Savoy incident. They also wanted a list of all the divers and boat crew. They said there was an ongoing investigation."

"Did they say why they wanted all that stuff?"

"Yeah. They said it was a shark attack investigation."

"A shark attack! You've got to be joking. The FBI doesn't investigate shark attacks."

"You and I and a few others know that, but John Q. Public doesn't. So, considering it involved a high-profile scientist and the project sparked considerable international interest, they probably wanted to spin the accident on a more plausible culprit."

"We'll talk about this later. I've got work to do in the lab. See ya."

****

Seated at her microscope, Willow slipped on a pair of rubber gloves and placed the material she had discovered under her microscope. Using tweezers in both hands, she manipulated the sample under the optics and began to separate individual pieces of varying sizes, shapes, and composition. As she proceeded, she began to record her findings.

"The sample contains several strands of hair from two different humans. One is grey, the other is brown. There are several insect parts tangled in the hairs - three bodies and assorted legs. I'm removing the hair from the sample and continuing to examine the insect parts with greater magnification. The first body is virtually identical to the Pacific pelagic halobate, *H. sericeus,* but there are some distinctive anomalies." Quivering, Willow abruptly popped back from the microscope. Shaking her head, she considered the scientific significance of her observations, and the potential hazards if her discovery was revealed to contentious adversaries. Willow mumbled something about discretion being the better part of valor and continued to record her observations.

"The body is approximately fifteen millimeters long by four millimeters wide. Two rear legs and two middle legs are intact. The two front legs are missing as are the antennae. Anterior to the middle leg joints are two intact translucent wings, smaller, but similar to a mosquito. These wings do not appear to be capable of extended flight - rather they are more likely for achieving short-term airborne mobility." Erasing any doubts, she inspected her specimen under higher magnification and summarized her findings. "Contrary to the entomological specifications for halobates, the body of this insect has a pair of translucent wings."

Willow flinched at the sound of her own words and the possibility she was looking at either a mutation or a totally new species. Moments later, after regaining her equanimity, she continued her discourse. "As with the previous tardigrade and hagfish mutations, I believe these mutations could be caused by anomalies in DNA replication from exposure to toxic chemicals."

Enraptured with her discovery, Willow rose from her stool and took a short break. She stretched out her arms, bent over at the waist and touched her toes. Leaning back, she rotated her hips clockwise and performed a dozen jumping-jacks. Feeling invigorated, she returned to her microscope.

Manipulating the sample with tweezers, she brought the head of the insect into view.

"Jumping jellyfish!" Willow blurted. "Maybe this insect isn't what it looks like. Maybe it's a totally new species. By God, this little freak has a proboscis like a mosquito. This necessitates a Gram staining. Maybe this critter is an agent for a bacteria or virus."

****

Gram staining is a common technique for differentiating bacteria based on their cell wall components and making the bacteria easier to identify under a microscope. The first step is to culture a large colony of bacteria in a petri dish containing an agar substrate. Agar is a gelatinous solution extracted from red seaweed and formulated with nutrients to provide an ideal medium for most bacterial species to rapidly propagate. The staining process distinguishes between Gram-positive and Gram-negative by coloring bacteria cells either violet or red. Gram-positive bacteria stain violet. Gram-negative bacteria stain red and are usually more resistant or impossible to kill with antibiotics.

Moreover, in any colony of bacteria, there will be variations in immunity to antibiotics. Those that are less immune are killed by the appropriate antibiotics, leaving only the strongest to reproduce. These bacteria are inherently more immune than the previous generation and will pass that immune characteristic to the next generation, resulting in each successive generation being stronger and more resistant than its predecessor.

After culturing and Gram staining, Willow nervously placed the petri dish under the microscope. A large, bright red colony of rod-shaped, Gram-negative bacteria occupied the upper half of the agar petri dish. She took a few digital images under strong magnification, downloaded them to her database and entered the appropriate cross-referencing commands into her computer. Similar to a fingerprint database, the software cross-referenced the microscopic features of her specimen to every bacterium in the database.

"Holy halibut!" Willow belted. "I've got a hit. *Vibrio vulnificus* - flesh-eating bacteria."

****

Vibrio, a Gram-negative, rod-shaped, pathogenic bacterium, lives in marine environments, from brackish backwaters to popular beaches. It is closely related to the bacterium that causes cholera. Vibrio is an extremely virulent bacterium causing acute ulcerations of the skin and mouth, high temperature, and septic coma. The organism is difficult to treat with the strongest antibiotics and quickly develops into septicemia, septic shock, and death. The disease is known to infect men six times more frequently than pre-menopausal females. Regardless of gender, if not treated within forty-eight hours, death is imminent.

****

"Blake, I'm home." Willow hollered. "Are you in bed?"

There was no immediate answer.

It had been a long day - one Willow would remember her entire life. She still had to complete a genomic DNA test on the specimen in order to determine if it was a mutated halobate or a new insect species. But it was past midnight and she was mentally and physically exhausted.

"Hey." Blake stirred as she walked into their bedroom. "You're home late. Did you manage to discover some new worlds?" he chuckled.

"As a matter of fact, I think I'm on to something rather astounding. I still have some DNA work to complete, but if it turns out the way I expect, it could have unprecedented implications for mankind."

"Good or bad?"

"Horrifying. I found what appears to be a halobate, a small oceanic insect. It may be a new species. It has the physical characteristics of a halobate except for two major differences, small wings, and a proboscis."

"What so horrifying about that?"

"Mosquitoes are agents of malaria and many other lethal diseases. Tsetse flies are agents of sleeping sickness. They have wings and a proboscis. I ran a Gram stain to determine if my insect specimen was an agent for bacteria. Turns out it is carrying vibrio, a deadly, flesh-eating bacterium that lives in the ocean. It's classified as a Type III infectious pathogen by the CDC, much worse than MRSA. There have been numerous fatalities, mostly men. Apparently, premenopausal women produce enough estrogen to provide some degree of resistance. The CDC is working on an antibiotic, but as of now, they have no way to stop it."

"Do you know for certain this insect is a halobate?"

"No, but I'm going to complete a DNA test tomorrow. That will tell us if it's a halobate or some new species. Because of the huge volume of floating garbage, plastic bottles, and other debris, halobates are multiplying at an astronomical rate. If they're agents of vibrio, then we're on the precipice of a pandemic. Millions, maybe hundreds of millions of people could perish. And the closer humans live to the ocean, the greater the risk - particularly for men."

Blake bolted from his pillow, stunned by her apocalyptic comment.

"You know, regardless of whether you're right or wrong, that could be a perilous assertion. I hope you don't plan to announce it to the news media. Look what happened to the Butlers, and hundreds of others who've espoused global catastrophe. I love you too much. Please be careful. We both know there are some dark forces out there with even darker assassins." Blake gave Willow a loving kiss on her cheek.

"I'm not talking about global warming. That issue has been battered and debated to irrelevance for decades. It's hard to separate fact from fiction. And besides, if we humans are too dumb or blinded by our own arrogance to deal with the more pressing maladies facing humanity during the next ten or twenty years, then no one will be around to witness the great Arctic meltdown that may or may not happen in the next thousand years."

Blake fell back onto his pillow, watching Willow get ready for bed while thinking how beautiful she was not only as a woman but as a human being. "I want you to be a shining star as a marine biologist, but on this mission, I hope you're mistaken."

****

Willow was up and back to her lab before seven.

She nervously prepared her new discovery for a genomic DNA test. While waiting for the sequencer to spit out the analysis, she fixed herself a cup of hot coffee and turned on the morning news. Regardless of the channel, the dominant headline was about the never-ending civil unrest in Africa, Asia, India, and South America. Warlords were confiscating food supplies and selling them back to the local population at usurious prices. Amazon natives were at war over clear-cutting ranchers who were determined to find more grazing room for their cattle. Gold miners continued to poison shrinking water resources by dumping deadly cyanide and mercury into the rivers and lakes. Water wars raged on every continent, as safe drinking water became a high-valued commodity. Each month, hundreds of thousands of people died from starvation or thirst. There simply wasn't enough food or potable water to support ten billion growling stomachs. If you couldn't pay for it, you died.

****

The ding-a-ling of the sequencer grabbed Willow's attention and she rushed to learn the results. As the report spilled out, she let the paper flow evenly through her fingers, stopping from time to time to ascertain specific data points. Near the end of the printout was an asterisk. Next to it was the genomic name of the sample and a couple of footnotes.

"*H. sericeus*," Willow cried out. "A halobate from the Great Pacific Garbage Patch. If I hadn't seen it myself, I would have never believed it was possible."

She continued scanning the printout, hoping to find some additional data.

"Suffering sockeye!" Willow exclaimed. "Here's the footnote I was expecting. The sample contains sixteen percent foreign DNA. It's a mutation. And there's another footnote that indicates the presence of PCBs, polystyrene derivatives, and other toxins. I think I know what killed the men on the sailboat."

CHAPTER 14

THE RAINMAKER

For over a hundred years, Faiseur de Pluie, The Rainmaker, had been a storm cellar and drinking establishment for prominent soldiers of fortune, habitual mercenaries and storied men of ambiguous character.

Situated on a narrow Brussels alley off Violetstraat, to a stranger the inauspicious atmosphere most likely caused great trepidation. For over a hundred years, many unknowing visitors have blithely walked through her heavy doors, sniffed the subterfuge, and quickly departed.

It was past eight on a rainy fall evening when a tall, well-dressed, middle-aged man walked into the bar. He stored his umbrella and took a seat at a small table near the rear of the establishment. He waved two fingers to the bartender and placed his black fedora on the table. Parted down the middle of his head, his grey, slicked-back hair curled up behind his neck.

The bar was half-filled with men whose birth names were buried deep in the graves of their ancestors. Everyone, even the barkeeps, had earned a nickname, often based on previous exploits, physical attributes, or idiosyncrasies.

Here in this musty den of iniquity, Chatham House Rules were unmercifully enforced. Patrons were free to use whatever information they gleaned from the gatherings, but they were not allowed to divulge the identity, position, or affiliation of the speaker.

Volker knew the place well. He'd spent many hours sipping his favorite twenty-year-old, single-malt Scotch whiskey, soaking up its peaty aroma and allowing the temperate flavors to trickle down his throat while contemplating his next project.

Shortly, the barman delivered his drink. Volker took a taste and returned his glass to the table.

It wasn't long before his handler joined him and presented a manila envelope. Inside was a dossier containing a personal profile, photographs, education, habits, and daily routine of the target.

"How soon can you complete this project?"

Volker took a few minutes to review the dossier, then took another sip of his scotch. "How soon can you get me a first-class ticket to Hamburg?"

The handler handed him an envelope containing a first-class, round-trip airline ticket and twenty-five thousand dollars.

"I'll wire transfer the balance to your account when the project is complete."

"Agreed."

The handler nodded and left.

Volker didn't know precisely who was behind this project. It may have been The Group, the Commission, Big Pharma, or even the Council. He'd worked for each of them several times. It was nearly always the same scope of work - someone in a position of international prominence, a scientist or whiz-kid, or a well-intentioned whistleblower seeking to save the world from the greedy oligarchs preaching the New World Order.

CRAIG MARLEY

Volker didn't give a shit about who or why. It had to be someone or a group of someone's willing to take the ultimate measure necessary to protect their agenda. It might be agents of the Bilderberg Group, Trilateral Commission, or Council of Foreign Relations. It might be the Americans, EU, the Chinese, or Russians. To Volker, and most of his counterparts, he just wanted the adrenaline rush, the thrill of victory, and the money.

Volker was more secretive and frugal than most of his comrades. Many of the younger, less experienced professionals gloated in their conquests and quickly spent their money on fast cars and faster women. To these junior league wannabes, Volker was an icon. He had paid his dues, never failed to complete a project, kept a low profile, and had never become the subject of an investigation.

Even though he was often referred to as The Maestro, he often considered the possibility that one of these younger, opportunistic upstarts might try to take over his prestigious top-dog position. With that in mind, Volker was contemplating an early retirement, someplace warm and hospitable. He had accumulated millions and was tired of hiding in the shadows of purgatory.

Skilled in the art of murder for hire, Volker was masterful with all the tools of the trade, from small arms to booby traps. But his signature liquidation scheme, one that was virtually instantaneous and left no tell-tale markers, was a simple concoction, a mixture of fentanyl, a popular opiate-based street drug, and a couple of secret ingredients that tripled its potency. Three drops of his secret sauce could be painlessly delivered to the target through a high-powered auto-injector, exterminating the victim within seconds.

When the target was not easily approached, he equipped one of his custom-designed mini-drones with his radio-controlled auto-injector. These smart, silent drones allowed Volker to visually track his victim using thermal, daylight, or night-vision cameras. Using the smoothest possible propellers, perfectly balanced bearings, and shafts, Volker's mini-drones were so quiet they could spy on a nesting baby bird without disturbing the chick or the mother. The control module included GPS tracking and facial recognition software that provided an absolute identification of the target before and after the attack.

****

While seated comfortably on his flight from Brussels to Hamburg, Volker retrieved the manila envelope and scrutinized every detail about the target, his daily routine, favorite coffee house, restaurants, and habits.

According to his profile, his project was born and raised in Hamburg, the only son of a wealthy German shipbuilder. His mother had died shortly after he was born. At the age of four, his father had died of cancer, leaving his only offspring in the care of Gertie, the family governess. He led a pampered life and was driven to and from parochial schools until he went off to the University of Hamburg.

He had few friends and spent much of his time in the library or playing chess with a small gathering of upperclassmen while gaining a reputation for being a brilliant, albeit stubborn and eccentric, student. He excelled in mathematics, physics, and chemistry while earning a Master's degree in marine biology. Following his first oceanic expedition, he completed his PhD thesis on psychrophilic marine organisms, creatures that thrived in extremely cold or frozen environments - extremophiles.

Now, forty years later, he had published numerous peer-reviewed scientific papers on extremophiles, and participated in an undersea research project, living and working inside a sea-floor habitat in six hundred feet of water off the coast of Waimanalo, Hawaii.

****

He had just finished his pork roast dinner with potato dumplings and gravy when he caught the attention of the Hofbräuhaus waitress.

"Niche ein bier, bitte."

Without breaking stride, the waitress snatched his personalized half-liter stein and proceeded to the bar.

As he looked around the hall for someone familiar, the oompah band took to the floor in their traditional lederhosen, white shirts, suspenders, knee-high socks, and feathered Alpine hats. Forming up two abreast, the four musicians began to liven up the spirits of the rowdy crowd with the triple-time honking of two tubas accompanied by the organic bellowing from a pair of accordions. Not particularly interested in denatured music orchestrated to entertain the tourists, he would have preferred to leave, but he wasn't about to abandon the third stein of his favorite lager.

Meanwhile, enduring the drizzling precipitation, Volker waited in the shadows of the alleyway separating the Hofbräuhaus from a row of retail stores. Inside his right coat pocket, he gripped a cigarette-size, spring-loaded, stainless steel auto-injector containing precisely three drops of his proprietary deadly cocktail.

The light drizzle soon segued to a thick fog moving up the River Elbe from the North Sea. Volker looked up and smiled, thankful that his project was about to be complete.

Minutes later, the tipsy target exited the Hofbräuhaus, pulled the collar of his overcoat up to his ears and looked about for an available taxi. Seeing none, he decided the foggy conditions were tolerable and began to stumble toward his flat.

The *fait accompli* was over in a trice. With the speed and coordination of a ninja, Volker brushed past his target while simultaneously pressing the business end of the auto-injector against Walter's thigh. Volker continued walking down the street for several feet, but stopped to look back the moment he heard the body crumble to the concrete.

Volker exchanged the now empty auto-injector for his mini-camera, took a couple of close-up shots of the body, and disappeared into the Hamburg fog.

CHAPTER 15

A GANG OF DICK SWALLOWS

It was sunny Saturday morning when Willow walked into the kitchen and poured herself a cup of her favorite Kona coffee from the pre-programmed percolator. As she walked toward the kitchen table, she blew across the steaming liquid while inhaling its delicate aroma. She took a seat and picked up the phone.

Bill answered on the second ringtone. "Hello."

"It's me. I've got some new information and need your help."

"We need to talk in private. Can you come to Santa Barbara this coming Wednesday? Rent a car and drive north on 101 to El Capitan Beach. Call me when you arrive. I'll meet you there."

"See ya Wednesday." Willow terminated the call, buried her head in her cupped hands, closed her eyes, and massaged her forehead. Blake suddenly walked into the kitchen.

"What the matter, sweetie? You look troubled. You're working too hard. Maybe we should take that break we've been talking about." Blake placed his brawny hands over her shoulders and began to massage the muscles surrounding her neck.

"It's not about my work at the university. I've got to go to Santa Barbara on Wednesday. Bill Knight and I need to talk about these mysterious deaths." Willow loathed herself for misleading Blake but dared not tell him how deeply she had delved into the recent DNA mysteries.

****

The drive from the Santa Barbara airport to El Capitan Beach took about thirty minutes. Willow parked her car near the beach a few spaces down from an aging pickup truck and a four-wheel Jeep convertible. A hundred yards offshore, two surfers sat upright on their surfboards, facing offshore while wishing for the perfect wave to carry them to nirvana.

Moments later, Bill pulled into the lot and parked his vehicle next to Willow's rental. He opened the back door and his golden retriever, Jake, dashed across the parking lot to greet his friend from Hawaii.

Patting Jake on the head and scratching his neck, Willow called out, "Hi, Bill!"

"Hi, Willow. It's nice to see you. How's Blake?"

"Blake is Blake. The man is like a rock, always optimistic, never complains about my cooking, and he keeps me warm at night." Willow and Bill chuckled.

"Come, let's find a place to talk. I've got a couple of beach chairs. Let's walk down toward the water. I see you have a rather large briefcase."

"I've brought a few of my files for you."

After a few minutes of pleasantries and a moment to take in the majesty of the ocean, Bill broke the news.

"I've been fired."

"What the...! Naw, you're kidding, right?"

"Last week, I received a very formal letter, certified and hand delivered, from the law firm representing the university. It said my services were no longer required. And, in accordance with my contract, I will retain my pension and medical benefits."

"Did they explain why?"

"Nope. The wording was something about my contract allows the Chancellor to dismiss any employee at any time, without cause. There doesn't have to be a reason. What was even more perplexing is that none of my faculty, friends I've known for decades, would speak to me. I was dumbfounded and pissed."

Willow was caught completely by surprise; her jaw dropped and she gasped. "That's unbelievable. Christ, you've been tenured for twenty years. What are you going to do?"

"Actually twenty-two years, and I'm not going to do a damn thing about it."

"Now you're really scaring me."

"There's more. I've just learned that all my papers detailing extremophiles and DNA mutations have been declared invalid. The university has erased them from the school library and website and sent apologetic letters to the entire scientific community."

"That's absurd. Why the hell would they do a thing like that?"

"Good question, Willow. I can think of only one reason. They don't want to be complicit. And they don't want their masters to cut off their funding. They're claiming I was lying and was desperate for attention. They held a briefing with the professors and staff of the Marine Sciences department and told them I was demented and not to use my name or any of my past work as reference material."

Vigorously shaking, Willow could barely speak. "Dick swallows! They're just a gang of dick swallows."

Bill chuckled. "Where'd you come up with that euphemism?"

"It's British, or Scottish, or maybe Irish. I seldom use the English equivalent."

"Well, I don't mean to frighten you, but there have been some strange things occurring around the world. A few days ago I received a text message from one of the Deputy Directors of Woods Hole, an old friend. They're a private research institution, not a state university. We go back many years. It was a veiled warning. Apparently, some of my recent papers on extremophiles and DNA mutations didn't sit well with the mucky-mucks - the people who provide the millions of dollars of annual funding for the institution. My friend told me my research was contrary to their objectives and was no longer considered worthy of academic credibility."

"Do you think they know about the mutated tardigrades or hagfish?"

"I don't know if my phone was bugged. But I believe someone talked. Maybe it was Walter. He was the only other person besides me who witnessed the DNA tests we conducted while in the habitat. You called me and said you couldn't sleep because you were thinking about Karen Savoy and were trying to understand the cause of her death. Blake told you Doctor Joe gave me some samples of the organisms that attacked Karen."

"Well, since we're playing doctor, and you've shown me yours, I guess I have to show you mine." Willow opened her briefcase and removed her file folder. "It's all in there. Blake doesn't know the contents. One of my grad students helped with the first DNA test on the tardigrade. She promised me she would keep the data a secret. But who knows. Maybe she let it slip out. I haven't talked to her since we did the tests. But there's much more. I've got the files with me."

"I'll study the files later, but give me the short version."

"It all started when I received a call from the coroner in Kauai. He had received the body of a drowning victim whose skeletal remains were recovered off the coast of Ni'ihau. The coroner had saved a few of the organisms that were recovered from the body and wanted to know if I would be interested in analyzing them. My grad student and I discovered the organisms were mutated. The sequencer indicated the mutations were due to horizontal gene transfer - twenty-one percent. There was also a footnote that indicated the presence of PCBs, polystyrene derivatives, and other toxins. I assumed the source of these chemicals to be the Great Pacific Garbage Patch. But you also mentioned *E. stoutii*. What did hagfish have to do with Karen's death?"

For a moment, Bill was speechless, his eyes darting left to right, then skyward as if looking for an interloper. "You gotta be real careful these days. Goddamn spies are everywhere. My reference to hagfish was a result of the research Walt and I completed while in decompression. Karen was initially attacked by a school of hagfish. She had accidentally torn her dry suit and was bleeding from a small cut. The hagfish may have been attracted by the blood and swam inside her partially flooded suit. Doctor Joe believes they went into a feeding frenzy like piranhas and she probably died from loss of blood. However, a cloud of tardigrades - the mutated variety - drove off the hagfish and consumed all the soft tissues down to the bare bones. Doctor Joe retrieved some bits and pieces of hagfish and a few samples of our giant *dujardini*. Walt and I worked together to complete the DNA tests."

"Did you find anything unusual about the hagfish?"

"The mutations were obvious. The hagfish that attacked Karen had complex eyes, a lens, and extraocular muscles to move them. These creatures probably had peripheral vision and could focus on an object, even a moving target. Hagfish don't have complex eyes or extraocular muscles, and they can't resolve images. Anyone who saw this evidence first-hand could rightfully claim the organism was a mutation."

Willow took a deep breath and looked out to sea. After a long pause, she removed another folder from her briefcase.

"Oh, no. Don't tell me you've got more."

"Oh, yeah! There was a woman who apparently died from bloodworm poisoning. Doctor Joe learned of her death from an ER intern at the Kailua Hospital. Out of curiosity, Doctor Joe called the coroner's office. They said they had no record of the victim or a bloodworm death. Blake and I managed to capture a bloodworm from the same beach and I discovered it had mutated. Its fangs were longer and the poison was more deadly than a taipan. I told Blake I had some new information that may have unprecedented implications for mankind. He warned me to be careful, but I have to trust someone. You, Bill, I trust you."

"Are you sure you want to do this?"

"I've got to. It's in my genes." Willow snickered at the metaphor.

"There was a news story on television about a sailboat that foundered off the coast of the big island. The boat was headed to Hawaii from San Diego with five people, two men, two women and a young girl. The Coast Guard reported the two adult women and the teenage girl were the only survivors. You got that so far?"

Bill nodded and, with trembling fingers, scratched his graying temple.

"But here is where the story goes awry. The media report said the surviving women told the police that the men caught a couple of pufferfish and decided to eat them. The coroner said they died from tetrodotoxin poisoning because they failed to properly clean the fish. The sailboat was several hundred miles from Hilo when the Coast Guard received their Mayday. Bill, you and I both know there are no pufferfish in the middle of the Pacific."

"So the news story was bogus. Humm, fake news. That doesn't surprise me. Please continue." Bill motioned for more information.

"You know me. I've got too much curiosity in my brain. I couldn't let it go without double checking the story. I called the Hilo coroner and he basically told me to fuck off but confirmed the sailboat story. I then contacted the Coast Guard and told them I was interested in buying the boat. They let me inspect the exterior. *Justice* was her name - a beautiful sailboat out of San Diego. I also learned that the media story was issued three weeks *after* the funeral and the survivors had returned home. I thought that was highly suspicious. Anyway, I managed to gather some material from the boat and took it back to my lab for analysis."

"Let me guess. You found something worthy?"

"Halobates. The two men died after being bitten by halobates. Except these halobates were mutations - they had small wings and a proboscis similar to a mosquito or tsetse fly."

"What was the cause of death?"

"Vibrio, a Gram-negative, flesh-eating bacterium."

Bill sat in silence for several moments while Willow looked out at the surfers shuttling in and out of the breakers.

"Listen, Willow." Bill took hold of her arm. "I'm embarrassed to say this, but I'm not willing to join you on this crusade." Tears filled Bill's eyes as he continued. "You're a great friend and an inspirational scientific pioneer. I'm sure Blake loves you and needs you in his life. Humanity needs you too. Someday, whoever is left in this world will recognize your contributions. However, I now believe there is nothing you or I can do to prevent the battle from raging onward. I'm sorry, Willow. I can't help you."

****

"Honey, it's me," Willow shouted out as she opened the front door.

"Welcome back. How was your flight?" Blake gave Willow a long hug and a wet kiss.

"The flight was fine. Bill, on the other hand, not so. It's very disturbing. I need a drink. Come, let's go sit on the lanai and I'll tell you everything."

Blake mixed a couple of mai-tais and they each took a seat on the lanai looking out to sea. In between long pulls on her cocktail,

Willow proceeded to recount the information she and Bill shared during their meeting at El Capitan Beach.

"It appears someone knows the truth about my research," Willow surmised.

"Whomever it is has probably commenced a textbook disinformation campaign." Blake was familiar with these types of progressive shenanigans. It was a typical, deep-state disinformation strategy starting with denial, followed by fake news - discredit the source - intimidation, and if deemed necessary, elimination. "Does Bill believe someone squealed? He's a big advocate for you and your research."

"Yes. Somehow some information has been leaked. You're right about the disinformation campaign. Bill has been fired and his entire body of work is being discredited. He said he would no longer be involved. He said he thought it was too dangerous."

Blake looked at Willow like a kid who had just lost his dog. He took her hand in his, squeezing it gently.

"I've got some sad news. And, for better or worse, it fits into your perspectives perfectly."

Willow caught her breath and gathered up her emotions. "What now?"

"Walter Schmidt is dead. I received an email from one of his Hamburg University colleagues. They found his body on the sidewalk in front of the Hofbräuhaus. The police believe he had some sort of seizure. There were no witnesses and the case is considered closed. Frankly, the story stinks."

CHAPTER 16
JAEGGER AND STONECIPHER

The taxi driver must have had psychic powers as he managed to weave in and out of back alleyways of New York to reach the United Nations Building in record-setting time.

"Here, keep the change," Willow said as she struggled to exit from the compact electric taxi with her briefcase filled with her research documents.

The foyer was filled with men and women rushing in and out of the three rotating doors, each wiping the sweat from their forehead. Most of the men wore tailored suits and ties. A few others wore native attire from African or Middle East nations. It was ten past nine on a sweltering Wednesday morning.

Beads of perspiration from the oppressive humidity trickled down Willow's cheeks. She approached the reception and offered her passport and driver's license. "I have an appointment with Simeon Jaegger."

"Yes, here it is. You're cleared to proceed. Please wear this badge at all times. Take the elevator to your left, the fifteenth floor."

In addition to being a notable professor emeritus from Yale, Simeon Jaegger had earned a reputation as a tough, often foul, but open-minded business executive. He served on the board of directors for a number of international conglomerates and bankers. Early in his career, as an executive for the largest agricultural company in the world, he initially promoted the move toward genetically modified organisms, but eventually, for undisclosed reasons, changed his opinion and became an outspoken critic of GMO. He retired from the private sector shortly after the company was sold and entered the diplomatic corps, serving first as ambassador to Indonesia until his most recent assignment as Director of the United Nations Marine Resource Commission.

"Good morning, Doctor Parker. Welcome to New York. Please have a seat. I hope you can accustom yourself to this muggy climate. I'd much rather be in Honolulu myself. Can I get you a coffee, tea, water?"

"Coffee would be great, black please."

Jaegger poured two cups of coffee, handed one to Willow and took his seat in front of a large picture window overlooking the East River.

"I understand from our brief conversation that you have empirical, I think that's the word you used, empirical information, gathered through your personal experiments and first-hand observations regarding something to do with extremophile mutations."

"Yes, sir. That is exactly how I presented it to your secretary and in my introductory letter to you."

"I've read your letter. You have a large following, including, I believe, Doctor Bill Knight?"

"Yes, Bill and I have worked together. I'm delighted to learn you know him." Willow immediately felt compromised. Why would Jaegger mention Bill Knight?

"We're not drinking buddies, mind you. But I know of him." Jaegger pushed back into his leather chair and folded his hands across his lap. "I have a very busy schedule, so let's get down to business. Can you summarize your findings and proposal?" Jaegger looked at his watch as if he was already behind schedule.

Taking a notebook from her briefcase, Willow began to summarize the bullet points.

"Over the past several weeks, I've documented a number of mysterious deaths apparently caused by mutated extremophiles - organisms living in the toxic environment of the Great Pacific Garbage Patch. I'm sure you know the extent of the pollution. I'll break my findings down into categories. First is my scientific evidence.

"A Hawaiian free diver was killed by mutated tardigrades. DNA test confirmed the species. The mutation was caused by horizontal gene transfer due to plastic toxins. A few weeks later, during a deep diving expedition, Doctor Karen Savoy was attacked by a school of hagfish, possibly attracted by her blood. Her body was consumed by the hagfish and the mutated tardigrades. DNA of the hagfish indicated a mutation due to horizontal gene transfer from the toxic plastic environment. Next, two adult male sailors were killed off the coast of Hilo by a swarm of marine insects that invaded their sailboat. I conducted DNA and determined the creature that killed them was a halobate, a small marine insect that thrives in the Great Pacific Garbage Patch. It too had mutated and the DNA test confirmed the horizontal gene transfer due to the photodegraded plastic. Finally, I conducted a Gram test of the halobate and was astounded to see evidence of *Vibrio vulnificus*, a lethal, class three, flesh-eating bacterium. This otherwise harmless insect had developed wings and a proboscis and is now an agent of deadly bacteria. Finally, we had a mysterious death on an Oahu beach when a woman was killed by bloodworms. They too had mutated and now possess the most potent venom of any organism on the planet."

"You have all the proof, the DNA sequencing printouts, Gram test, and toxicology analysis?"

"Yes, sir. And there are eyewitnesses to some of the deaths. That's my next subject, witness intimidation, and fake news.

"The death of the Hawaiian diver was listed as accidental drowning. The death of Karen Savoy was officially declared a shark attack. The sailboat deaths were characterized as death due to ingestion of improperly prepared pufferfish. However, the vessel was reportedly inspected by a team of men dressed in hazmat attire and the interior was secured with a padlock by the Hilo PD. As regards the bloodworm death, the Kauai coroner has no record of the incident. Finally…" Willow hesitated, wondering if she should take her recital to the next level. "Bill Knight indicated he was terminated from his professorship at UCSB due to dementia. The university disavowed his credentials, claiming his volumes of research papers were no longer accepted as valid reference material. Let me assure you, sir. Bill Knight is not suffering from dementia. Frankly, he told me he was afraid for his life."

"I'm sorry to hear about Bill. But that's not my problem. If what you are telling me is true, we have a very serious problem. However, as you know, this kind of data must undergo a lengthy peer review process. Moving forward toward confirmation of your work can take years. And if the problem is confirmed, there's no way to pinpoint the responsible parties and there are certainly no financial resources to fix it."

"That's my primary reason for this visit, to see if you can use the power and prestige in your official capacity as Director of the Marine Resources Commission to expedite the peer review and initiate a funding effort. It could take hundreds of billions or more, but someone has to take the lead. I was hoping it would be you."

Jaegger leaned forward. Placing his cupped hands on his desk he gave Willow an apathetic stare. "Can you provide me with copies of your research?"

"Certainly. I have copies of all my work."

"Listen, I'm intrigued by our meeting and your observations. But, and I say this with all due respect, five mysterious deaths is not an earth-shaking event. In the United States alone, three hundred people die each year due to lightning, a handful perish from shark attacks. A dozen die from snake bites. People still play golf during thunderstorms and surf in shark-infested waters."

"But sir, this is not a golf course or Malibu. We're talking about a floating island of toxic waste *eight times the size of Alaska*."

"I understand your concerns, Parker. And I appreciate your bringing it to my attention." Jaegger cocked his head and raised his right index finger. He picked up his phone and quick-dialed a long-distance number.

"Hello, Bea. This is Jaegger. I'm just wrapping up a meeting with Doctor Willow Parker. She's developed some interesting data on mutated marine organisms. One, in particular, may be an agent of Vibrio. I thought, if you had some time tomorrow, perhaps Doctor Parker could pay you a visit."

Jaegger listened for a few moments and then concluded the call.

"That was Doctor Beatrice Stonecipher. She's the Director of Emerging Zoonotic Infectious Diseases at the CDC in Atlanta. She said to come to her office after three tomorrow afternoon." Jaegger stood and waved toward the door.

"Thank you, Doctor Jaegger. I appreciate your time."

Jaegger stood and walked around his desk. Taking Willow by the arm, he gently, but firmly, escorted her from his office. "You're quite welcome. Good luck."

****

Doctor Beatrice Stonecipher had been with the CDC for over twenty years. She began her career as a principal investigator and worked her way up the chain of command to a directorship. Through the rumor mill, Willow had heard she was an eccentric, middle-aged woman with a dark, almost witchy personality. Having earned doctorate degrees in organic biology and zoonotic infectious diseases from Georgia Tech, she was inarguably qualified to hold her esteemed position.

"Good afternoon, Doctor Stonecipher." Willow held out her hand.

Stonecipher quickly responded, "Please take a seat."

Willow did her best to type-cast her quirky behavior. The first thing she noticed was the coal-black hair coiled up in a bagel-size bun at the back of her head. She wore a black, skin-tight skirt, a long-sleeved white silk blouse, and black high heels. Her thin lips were painted dark burgundy, as were her long, manicured fingernails.

"Jaegger told me you had some research data on Vibrio."

"Yes, that is right. I have a copy of my findings here." Willow passed Stonecipher her Vibrio report. "It began with my discovery of rapid mutations in some marine organisms living in the Great Pacific Garbage Patch. The DNA sequencer attributed these mutations to the toxicity of their environment - photodegraded plastics. One organism, a halobate, grew a set of wings and a proboscis. My Gram test indicated this particular marine insect was an agent of Vibrio. I believe it caused the death of two men while they were sailing off the east coast of the Big Island of Hawaii."

"Sailing off the coast of Hawaii? How interesting. Has anyone else witnessed your work or read your reports?"

"I gave copies to Doctor Jaegger and Doctor Bill Knight."

Stonecipher looked up at the ceiling, and then back to Willow. "I don't have time to review this immediately, and I have an urgent meeting scheduled. I'll get back to you," Stonecipher said with a smarmy grin.

Stonecipher walked from her desk and approached her receptionist. "Glenda, please escort Doctor Parker to the elevator."

CHAPTER 17

SHUT UP OR ELSE

The summer sun was about to break above the horizon when Blake opened his eyes and focused his attention on Willow's beautiful face peeking out from under her pillow. Willow was lost in her dreams, but as Blake continued his rhapsodic gaze, she felt a stirring and opened one eye.

"Hey, handsome," Willow whispered with an enticing smile.

"Good morning, sweetheart. I've been watching you sleep. You look so beautiful and peaceful. Were you dreaming?"

"Yeah. It was you and me on the beach somewhere in the South Pacific. We were cuddling by a fire, all alone under the stars. I think we were marooned on an uninhabited island but we had everything we needed to be happy. The water was a light blue, gulls dashed across the white sandy beach. Oh, it was so breathtaking." Willow moved closer, wet her lips and gave Blake one of her alluring mushy kisses on his lips. Blake reached out and gently touched her breasts while Willow commenced her captivating effleurage.

"I love you," she whispered.

"I love you too. I couldn't live without you."

"Life is so good when we're together," she whispered. "I can tell you're getting in the mood."

"I'm definitely in the mood for you. It's rather obvious, isn't it?"

"I love making love with you in the morning."

"Anytime is fine with me."

"Oh, blimey. Come shiver me timbers, Captain." Rolling over to receive her lover, Willow cooed. "Come softly to me. Whisper sweetness in my ear."

Their bodies slowly merged under the comforter - each of them knowing what the other wanted - what their lover needed. It was slow and deliberate - a perfectly beautiful union. The power of their love had no equal.

****

Drained of energy and awash in a sea of tranquility, Willow and Blake drifted off to a silky-smooth dreamscape for several minutes. Blake rolled to his side and gently kissed Willow on the cheek. Willow came face to face with Blake and kissed him on the lips. "That was fabulous. You numba one lover boy. Makee whoopi long time. Me love you long time."

"How'd it go at your meeting with Jaegger?" Blake broke the libidinous trance.

"Blimey, Captain. I thought we might do it one more time."

"Sorry. How about tonight? I've got to rehydrate."

"Okay. But I'm holding you to your word."

"So tell me about your big meeting."

"It didn't go well. Jaegger gave me about five minutes to summarize my findings. He said the mysterious death of five people was no big deal. He did ask me to leave my reports with his secretary, but I think he was just being polite. He referred me to one of his colleagues at the CDC. I had to go to Atlanta on the red eye. It was probably a waste of time. Doctor Beatrice Stonecipher. That was her name. Director of Emerging Zoonotic Infectious Diseases. She had the personality of a honey badger. In fact, now that I think about it, she even looked like a honey badger. She seemed to care less. She said she'd review my reports and get back to me."

"What's your next move?"

"You asked me that question before. I was thinking of going into hibernation, to continue with my teaching and keeping my mouth shut. Now that I have undeniable proof of what's going on, no one wants to hear it. And if I keep it up, they'll probably do their best to shut me up, like they did with Bill Knight and maybe Walter Schmidt. When you first asked me that question some time ago, you said you understood my feelings and I assumed you had no objections."

"At that time, I didn't think there were any hazards. And I believe your theories are correct. You have the data to support the story. However, now that I know what happened to Bill and Walter, and the brush-off by Jaegger and the CDC, I'm actually quite concerned. Why don't you take a break? Think about your options for a few weeks before making a decision. Let's take that vacation we've been talking about. I'll make reservations at the Royal Chateau."

CHAPTER 18

THE WHISTLEBLOWER

Blake unlocked the door to their home and struggled to maneuver the largest of four suitcases into the foyer. Willow followed, carrying her purse, a shoulder bag, and a small carry-on.

"That was some landing. I could hardly tell when we hit the runway. I'm going to open up some windows, let the sea breeze cool this place down. I had a great time in Chuuk, but it's always a joy to come home."

"Okay, you open up the windows; I'll get the rest of the luggage."

Willow walked into their bedroom, sat on the edge of the bed and checked the voicemail. There were four messages.

"Hi, Willow. Sammy here. Give me a call. I need to ask you about the royalty for your podcast. Hope you and Blake had a great time in Chuuk."

"Hello, Willow Parker. Your VISA card will expire on the last day of August. A new card has been sent. Please discard your old card and activate your new one."

"Doctor Parker. I need to speak with you as soon as possible. It's about the CDC. It is urgent. Please call me on my private line 404-555-5454."

Willow sensed there was something ominous in the shadows. Why else would an anonymous person from CDC call her and leave a cryptic message? And the message from Bill left her with an uneasy feeling. Her hands began to shake as she dialed the number. It was Saturday, six in the morning in Atlanta, Georgia.

"Hello."

"Hello. This is Doctor Parker. Did you leave a message on my voicemail?"

After a short pause, a male voice replied, "Can you talk?"

"Yes."

"Call me on my encrypted cell. 606-555-3765."

Willow keyed a fresh dial tone and entered the number.

"Don't say anything. Just listen. I'm an IT engineer at CDC. I work with Stonecipher on the Vibrio Project. I read a copy of your report. The two women and the daughter, the ones from the sailboat, are being held here, level four. They're being used as guinea pigs because they somehow survived a vibrio attack. Level four is the most secure and biologically safe area for testing antibiotics on emerging zoonotic infections. Everything you thought you knew about the incident is bullshit, CDC propaganda. Vibrio has the highest priority and is a lethal, pandemic threat to the entire planet. It thrives in fresh and salt water. No other bug comes close to the virulence of this organism. We have no treatment. Nothing works. Several years ago, we had some success with intravenous doxycycline with ceftazimide. But, within a few months, it became resistant and we are out of options. I don't know if this information will help your cause, but I felt compelled to let you know the facts. Please don't try to call me. I'm leaving Atlanta and the CDC. Good luck." The line went dead.

Like a bolt of lightning, a burst of adrenaline-laced panic raced through her head, down her back and stomach. Dizzy, she stumbled to the bathroom. Dropping to her knees, she puked several times before regaining some sense of equanimity.

"Willow, are you ill? Can I help?"

"Uuhhgg. Whew. Sorry, I just lost it. It must have been something I ate. I'll be okay."

"Here, let me help you onto the bed."

"Okay. Let me rest for a few minutes. It's probably just from all the excitement and the long flight home."

CHAPTER 19

A DOUBLE HEADER

Volker held the door open with his right foot while pushing his umbrella through the doorway of the Faiseur de Pluie. A storm front had moved in over Brussels, dumping several inches of chilling rain over her cobblestone streets.

A few of the usual customers sat at the bar or at their usual table, drinking their favorite Trappist beer, Irish, or malt Scotch whiskey.

It was almost ten when Volker hung up his umbrella and raincoat and took a seat at his preferred table near the rear of the noisy establishment. As was his customary signal, he waved two fingers to the bartender and placed his black fedora on the table. Rainwater dripped from the ends of his curly hair.

The bar was more noisy than usual and the crowd included the crew from an ocean-going tug tied up at the wharf awaiting calmer seas before heading into the North Sea in support of a deepwater oil drilling operation. The revelers were well on their way to an all-nighter when the barman delivered Volker's drink.

"Good evening, sir. It's good to see you again. Can I get you something to eat?"

Volker tossed the barman a few euros and gestured to him to depart.

Shortly, Volker took a sip of his single-malt scotch and settled his glass on the table.

A few minutes later, his handler joined him.

"Good evening. We have, as American baseball fans say, a double-header. Here are their dossiers." The handler handed him one of the envelopes.

Volker opened the first envelope. Inside he found the dossier of his first project. He carefully read the documents and photographs while sipping his scotch. When finished with the first dossier, he returned it to the envelope. He then opened the second envelope and reviewed its contents.

"Everything seems to be in order. You are aware there is no discount for, as you put it, a double-header?"

"Absolutely. Your fees will be wired to your account upon proof of completion of your assignments. Here is your down payment and first-class, round-trip tickets for both projects."

"Agreed!" Volker said as he placed the envelope containing the cash and tickets in his jacket pocket.

The handler took a moment to collect his thoughts, and then asked Volker a question. "Please do not be offended. We've been meeting like this for several years, but how did you get into this business?"

"I don't really like to talk about it. But I will tell you the short version. I was once a member of a secret team within the German Special Forces. Our job was to seek out and kill or capture Muslim terrorists. We were a very effective gang and we seldom took prisoners. One day, my father and mother were kidnapped by a local terrorist cell. It was in Cologne, where I was born and raised. They wanted money, a ransom. I arranged for the ransom to be paid. Instead of returning my parents, they brutally beheaded them on camera and posted the video on their website. I had to avenge their deaths. It took two years, but I sought out each of the perpetrators and…now you know the story."

"But these targets are not Muslims."

"Killing can be habit-forming. It produces a high. And regardless of race, creed or color, it's all about the money and the euphoria."

"Are you ever going to retire? You must have plenty of money."

"Maybe. I'm thinking about it. You'll be the first to know."

"I don't understand the brain chemistry, but thanks for the explanation. See you next time." The handler turned and departed.

****

Like all of his previous projects, Volker didn't know precisely who was behind this project. He'd worked for many organizations, mostly men of influence and power, men who needed him to do their bidding. He really didn't care. The money provided a profitable return for the risk and he loved the thrill of the kill.

Volker had paid his dues and was dedicated to being the best in every aspect of his work. In his earlier days, it was all guns with silencers or a sudden push out of an open window. Today, it was much stealthier. Murder for hire was a technology-driven enterprise, hi-tech in every sense of the word. Guns were for beginners, and they often got caught. Volker, on the other hand, had perfected his own weapon of choice. It was quick, silent, and foolproof.

****

Upon landing at the Los Angeles International Airport, Volker clutched his carry-on bag, cleared customs and immigration. He then took the airport shuttle to the domestic terminal where he joined one of several lines of passengers suffering the indignities of airport security. It was six o'clock in the evening.

As he approached the TSA checkpoint, he placed his carry-on bag on the conveyor, took off his shoes and belt and placed them in the white plastic bin.

"ID and boarding pass," the TSA officer barked. "Step forward for the body scan."

The officer gave him a dismissive smile, then scribbled his initials on his boarding pass and cleared him through the checkpoint.

Looking up, he saw the flashing neon sign above the bar and decided he needed a drink before his next flight.

"Double Lagavulin Gold," he ordered. "Neat."

The barkeep placed a white napkin on the bar and quickly returned with his drink.

Volker picked up the glass, held it up to the west-facing window and let the light of a setting sun reflect the amber color of his whiskey.

He then downed a large portion of his drink and retrieved the manila envelope of his first of two projects. Opening the dossier, he scrutinized the profile of a fifty-nine-year-old man, a retired University of California professor living in Santa Barbara. He studied the remaining information and photographs for a few minutes, and then ordered another double scotch.

****

Willow suddenly burst upright from her pillow, the aftermath of her premonition still burning inside her thoughts.

"Are you okay?" Blake asked in a drowsy undertone.

"I had a bad dream. What time is it?"

"Four-thirty. What kind of a dream was it?"

"It was about Bill. He was walking Jake, his golden retriever, on the El Capitan beach. Suddenly a huge wave, maybe a tsunami, washed across the beach, sweeping Bill and Jake out to sea. I wonder if there's some hidden meaning to that dream."

"There's one way to find out. Give him a call. It's seven-thirty in Santa Barbara."

"Great idea, Blake."

Willow picked up her smartphone and dialed Bill's number. With each successive ringtone, her mindset devolved from optimism to concern to trepidation. The automatic voicemail greeting commenced on the sixth ringtone.

"Leave a message. I'll return your call as soon as possible."

****

It was late afternoon when Volker returned to Los Angeles. Having completed the first project, he now looked forward to his next flight. It would give him time to prepare his mind for the second game of his double-header. With no time to dawdle, he rushed to the departure gate where the first-class passengers were already boarding. He handed his boarding pass to the gate attendant and quickly found his seat next to a window. After stowing his carry-on bag in the overhead bin, he settled into his seat.

"May I get you a cocktail?" the stewardess asked.

"Double Lagavulin Gold, neat."

"I'm sorry. We only carry Glenfiddich."

Displeased, Volker replied, "That will have to do."

Shortly, a tawny male passenger approached the aisle seat, stored his bag and settled into the aisle seat next to Volker.

"Good afternoon. I'm Rafael," he said, offering his right hand.

Volker looked into Rafael's eyes for several heartbeats, and then replied, "Thanks. I'm just fine."

Rafael quickly recoiled from the obvious rebuff and fastened his seatbelt.

After finishing his drink, Volker ordered another.

"I'll have the same as this gentleman," Rafael said to the stewardess.

While sipping his drink, Volker removed a travel magazine from the seatback pocket. Inside, page after page described an assortment of picturesque beaches from the Bahamas, to the South Pacific. Each touted the beauty of pristine beaches, the laid-back lifestyle, exciting nightlife, gourmet food, wine and exotic accommodations. From the images of the featured vacation hot-spots, one could imagine there were lusty bikini-clad ladies at every location. He envisioned himself on the beach, talking to a pair of sex kittens, fondling their breasts and enjoying their charms. The thought of retiring in one of these tropical settings was intoxicating.

****

Shortly after takeoff, Volker ordered another drink. The alcohol helped bring to life each step in his next project. Like a virtual world with live avatars, Volker relied on his instincts and experience to bring into focus the landscape - the setting - his point of insertion - the unaware victim - the moment of truth, and his extraction.

Rafael broke the spell. "Do you live in Los Angeles?"

"No." Volker shook his head

"I'm from Portugal. I'm taking some time off."

"Portugal. I thought so. It's your accent."

"My family owns several olive groves north of Lisbon, near Fatima. Have you ever heard of Fatima?"

"Fatima? That's where three shepherd kids saw an apparition of the Virgin Mary. It was on October 13, 1917. It's called the Miracle of the Sun."

"Hey, I'm really impressed. Not many people know about Fatima."

Rafael continued to talk, recounting stories about his grandfather, a decorated, three-star general in the Portuguese army, and his conquests during the colonial wars in Africa.

After an hour or more of Rafael's prattle, Volker had heard enough. "Sorry, Rafael, but I need to catch some sleep. Don't wake me up until we're on the ground."

"Sure. No problem."

Volker rested his head against a small pillow, closed the window shutter, pushed his seatback to the fullest reclined position and soon fell into a deep sleep.

****

Rafael reached into his pocket and removed a ball-point pen and a small notebook. He proceeded to write a few scribbles until he was certain his next few moves would go unnoticed. He unscrewed the top half of the pen and removed a red plastic tube - an exact replica of an airline cocktail straw.

Turning his back to the aisle, he placed the open end of the plastic tube over the lip of Volker's empty cocktail glass. He then squeezed the tube between his thumb and index finger crushing a thin glass capsule buried inside the tube. Several colorless, odorless and tasteless drops of supercharged fentanyl, formulated to Volker's own recipe, slithered to the bottom of Volker's glass. Rafael then poured the contents of his glass into Volker's and placed the red plastic tube into his empty glass.

"May I get you another drink, sir?" The stewardess asked, seeing Rafael's empty glass.

"No, thanks. But you may dispose of this one."

****

"Ladies and gentlemen. Please bring your seat to an upright position and fasten your seatbelt. We will be landing soon."

Rafael pushed the button on Volker's seat, bringing it to the proper position.

"Hey, what's up?" Volker awoke, groggy but aware of his surroundings. "Are we landing?"

"Yeah. You'd better finish your scotch. They'll be picking up the glasses any minute."

Volker reached for his scotch and downed it in one large gulp. As if slapped in the face by an insulted starlet, he shook his head and blinked several times. Seconds later, his eyes momentarily burst open like a crazed madman's, and then slowly closed. His head fell against the airline pillow with a muffled thump.

After making a textbook landing, the aircraft came to a full stop at the terminal.

"Ladies and gentlemen, you are now free to move about the cabin and collect your luggage."

Rafael hurriedly grabbed Volker's carry-on bag and was the first passenger to reach the exit door.

"The Captain and crew would like to thank you for flying with us today. The outside temperature is seventy-five degrees. Welcome to Honolulu."

About the Author

Craig is a former Navy SEAL, Vietnam vet, and a pioneer in the deep-sea diving industry. His underwater adventures have taken him to the deepest and most hostile parts of the world's oceans. He's worked with bottlenose dolphins, undersea habitats, submersibles, remote-controlled underwater vehicles, and experimental diving equipment. His most recent books take the reader on a magical journey into the world of predictive science-fiction. Grounded in empirical scientific and technological advances, his epic thrillers provide insight into the breakthroughs and tribulations mankind may encounter during the next twenty years.

Craig lives in Southern California with his wife, Lynn.

OTHER BOOKS BY CRAIG